Little Things

Books by Donya Lynne

All the King's Men Series
Rise of the Fallen
Heart of the Warrior
Micah's Calling
Rebel Obsession
Return of the Assassin
All the King's Men – Prequel
Bound Guardian Angel

Strong Karma Series
Good Karma
Coming Back To You
Full Circle

Standalones
Finding Lacey Moon
Little Things

M/M Standalones
Winter's Fire

Writing as Dick Hertz
Size Matters, Parts 1-8

Little Things

Donya Lynne

Little Things
Donya Lynne
Copyright © 2016 Donya Lynne
ISBN: 1-938991-21-4
ISBN 13: 978-1-938991-21-9

Cover art by Pink Ink Designs
Edited by Laura LaTulipe

Acknowledgements

Writing books is one of the hardest, most rewarding things I've ever done, and like raising a child, every book takes a village. From the readers to my editor to my cover artist, and to all the wonderful authors, reviewers, and bloggers I've met along the way, my village is full of amazing, enormously talented people. Far too many to name. If I tried, I'm afraid I would leave someone out. Just know that I appreciate every last one of you from the bottom of my heart.

A special thanks to Cassy Roop and Pink Ink Designs for the absolutely perfect cover for this story, and to my editor, Laura LaTulipe, who's been with me from the very beginning of my writing journey, even before I wrote the first word of my first book. May we work on many more projects together.

"Little things make big things happen."
-John Wooden

Chapter 1

"Are they here yet?" I call as I blow through the front door.

I drop my car keys and book bag on the couch then rush into the kitchen, where my mom is pulling golden-brown shortbread cookies from the oven. They're shaped like snowmen and Christmas trees.

She closes the oven door and gives me what I call her pacifying mom look. Her head is tilted to one side, her eyebrows raised. The appeasing grin that curls her lips is the one she's worn for as long as I can remember. The one that says she's learned she can't dissuade my overly eager anticipation and has accepted it as part of my genetic makeup, even though it occasionally gets on her nerves.

"Are they here yet?" I ask again as I drop my Highland Creek letter jacket on a barstool and dip my finger in a bowl of red frosting.

The arched brow and cockeyed smile my mom gives me bleeds amused impatience. "Did you see your brother's car in the driveway?"

I suck the frosting off my finger. I hate when my

mom answers a question with a question. "No, but that doesn't mean they're not here. They could have been here and left to go get something to eat."

My mom transfers the hot cookies to a cooling rack. A large platter of elaborately decorated cookies already sits at the end of the counter. Knowing how my mom channels the holiday spirit better than Santa Claus, she's probably been baking and decorating all day.

She gives me another of her mom looks. The one that says she knows why I'm so interested in whether my brother and his best friend are here, yet. "No, Cameron," she says in a slightly singsong voice, "Nick and Gunner haven't arrived, yet. You still have time to do your hair and makeup and change into that pretty new outfit you bought last week." She smiles knowingly as she begins rolling out another batch of cookie dough.

Busted.

I bite the inside of my bottom lip to keep from smiling, feeling the heat infiltrate my cheeks.

"Go on," my mom says. "Get changed. And you'd better hurry. I have a feeling they'll be here any minute."

"Why do you say that?"

"Nick texted a couple hours ago." She sets aside her rolling pin and grabs a Christmas tree cookie cutter. "They were a little over two hours away. So you'd better hurry if you want to look good for

Gunner." She winks.

A rush of electricity flies through me. He's almost here.

I slide off the barstool, my heart beating so hard at the thought of seeing Gunner again that it's a wonder I don't pass out. "I have no idea what you're talking about."

My mom rolls her eyes and laughs. "Sure you don't."

With a giggle, I steal a cookie from the platter and dart out of the kitchen, taking the stairs two at a time to my bedroom. I bring up the music app on my phone, and within seconds, Joe Jonas is blasting through my Bluetooth speaker, singing about eating cake by the ocean.

The new outfit I bought specifically for today is hanging in the front of my closet. I snag it from the rack and toss it on my bed before running into the Jack-and-Jill bathroom that connects my room to my older sister's. Wendy moved out a couple of years ago, though, and we've converted her room to a guest room, so the bathroom is more or less mine now. Which is awesome. What eighteen-year-old girl doesn't want her own bathroom?

I turn on the shower then strip out of my school clothes like they're on fire before stepping under the falling water. My hands are actually shaking as I fumble for the bottle of floral-scented body wash and squeeze out a generous dollop on my loofah.

I've been in love with my brother's best friend, Gunner, since the sixth grade, when he came over to play basketball with Nick one night after school. His family had just moved into the neighborhood, and it was the first time I saw him. And what an impression he made. Shirtless. Shooting hoops with Nick. I stared out the window from the upstairs study nook for over an hour, watching him. I haven't been able to look at another boy since.

What's not to love about Gunner? Eyes the color of the ocean at midnight under a full moon. Thick, dark-brown hair that's always a little mussed in a way that makes me want to comb my fingers through it. A body that's long and lean in all the right ways. And a straight-toothed smile that makes his dimples pop when he laughs.

He's perfection. Absolute, hot-bodied perfection.

If only I could catch his eye as something other than Nick's baby sister. I have a feeling that no matter how old I get, I'll always be "little Cami" to Gunner.

But I want him to see me as Cameron, his best friend's hot sister. Cameron, the gorgeous woman little Cami grew into.

I turned eighteen last month, so I can call myself a woman now.

The point is, that's how I want Gunner to see me. As a woman. Not the gangly, dorky, freckle-faced kid he met six years ago. Back then, I was boobless, hipless, and clueless.

In a lot of ways, I still am clueless, but at least my curves have come in. A little late, but better late than never. Having to wear the equivalent of a training bra until the beginning of junior year was mortifying. Talk about a nightmare in the locker room. Undressing in front of thirty other girls who all had big — at least big compared to me — perky breasts after gym class was my least favorite part of the day during sophomore year. Now I'm a senior, and I'm not so gun-shy around the other girls. My boobs may not be what could be called big, but they are perky.

And I love them. When I look at them in the mirror, I understand why guys are so fascinated with them.

Not mine, of course. I'm talking about boobs in general. No boys have seen mine, yet. I've sort of been saving them for Gunner. Crazy, I know, since he's shown absolutely no interest in me. But I can't help it. He's the only boy I want.

But I can't technically call him a boy, anymore, especially when he'll be twenty next month. Gunner's a man. A full-grown, oh-my-God-he's-so-hot man.

He's also a Capricorn. I'm a Scorpio. According to the astrology books I read when I was younger, that means we're compatible. I already know this. Now I need him to see it.

The good news is that the last time I texted with my brother, he said Gunner broke up with the girl he'd been dating at Ohio State. She was a Libra.

Totally incompatible with a Capricorn. I'm not surprised they didn't work out.

And I'm not surprised the other girls before her didn't work out, either. None of them are as good for him as I could be.

Maybe I'm being a little neurotic. But I just know Gunner and I would be good together. We both like basketball, listen to the same music, think science fiction movies are the best, and have quirky senses of humor. And we're both honor roll students. At least, Gunner was before he graduated two years ago and went to college.

The problem is, Gunner has his pick of the litter. His status at Highland Creek High School was so legendary that half the girls there are still in love with him. He and Nick are sophomores at Ohio State now, but that doesn't mean Gunner stopped being the dream of every girl living in Highland Creek.

And he's spending Christmas break at our house.

I'm the luckiest girl on earth.

After drying off, I wrap my towel around me and begin combing my hair, humming along with Ariana Grande's "Into You" as it blares from my room. My hair is long and thick, and I wasn't exactly gentle when I washed it, so it's more tangled than usual, but I quickly tame it.

I'm about to take off my towel and rush back to my bedroom to get dressed when the door to Wendy's room opens.

I spin, wide-eyed, holding the towel over the front of my body as I come face-to-face with Gunner.

My breath catches as my gaze locks to his.

"I'm sorry, I . . ." He begins to back away then stops as his gaze steamrolls down my body. "I didn't know you were in here."

I can't speak. All I can do is stand in the middle of my bathroom, frozen, with only a towel and a lot of empty air separating us.

His gaze climbs my legs, then lands on the towel as if he can see through it. He blinks as his eyes meet mine again, and his eyebrows pinch curiously over the bridge of his nose.

He's even better looking than he was the last time I saw him, which was back in August, before he and Nick packed the car and returned to Ohio State for the new term. His hair is shorter, but still mussed. Still thick. Still touch-me sexy. And the shadow of a trimmed beard outlines his jaw. That's new. I've never seen him with facial hair. I like it. It's dangerous in a sexy way.

He's bigger, too. Not fat. Muscular. He looks like a fitness model. Just . . . wow. His sculpted biceps stretch the fabric of his short sleeves, and his jeans hang more loosely than I remember from his tapered waist. The veins on his hands and forearms are even more pronounced, as if he's trimmed off a layer of body fat.

Looks like Gunner has definitely lost his freshman

five and then some, but damn, every time I see Gunner, he grows more good-looking. More like a man.

What am I saying? He *is* a man.

He blinks again, and it's like he's waking up from a daze. He hooks his thumb over his shoulder, which makes his biceps pop. I might have just drooled a little. "I'll just, uh . . . I'll use the hall bathroom."

The door shuts with an abrupt click, and, just like that, he's gone.

I let out the breath I didn't realize I was holding.

I didn't say a word. Not hello. Not how are you. Not it's nice to see you again. Not even it's okay that you barged in on me while I was practically naked.

Like a silly teenager, I remained mute in the face of what could have been a revolutionary moment.

But I think he finally saw me. *Really* saw me.

Maybe now I won't just be Nick's baby sister anymore.

Chapter 2

Dinner is about as comfortable as being rubbed with steel wool. After what happened in my bathroom, I can't even look at Gunner, although I can feel him watching me.

I dare a peek at him from the corner of my eye between nibbles of mashed potatoes. For a heartbeat, our gazes meet, and then he glances down at his plate.

Meanwhile, my mom and dad are blathering on about all the holiday parties they need to attend in the next couple of weeks. Not only does Dad's work hold a huge gala every December, but just about every organization my mom does charitable work for is having a party, too. They'll be lucky if they spend more than two nights at home between now and Christmas Eve.

Across from me, Nick is texting his girlfriend, who he hasn't seen since August. Every couple of minutes, he grins or lets out an amused snort. I'm sure they'll be spending a lot of time together now that he's home.

"How's school?" Gunner says, his deep voice cutting through the chatter.

I look up, surprised to realize he's talking to me. But who else would he ask about school? My parents? Not. And he probably sees Nick every day and doesn't need to ask him how school's going.

I gnaw my bottom lip as I feel my face heat. "Fine."

"Still playing basketball?"

I nod.

"She's the team's leading scorer," my mom chimes in with a wink my way.

Gunner's eyebrows lift as he sits a little taller. "I'm impressed. Must be all the times you played hoops with Nick and me." He bobs his head in the direction of the half court in the backyard.

"Maybe," I say quietly.

Funny how when he's not around, I can think of a million witty things to say, but when he is, my brain and my voice take a vacation.

I've been plagued with horrible shyness all my life, which is crazy for someone as competitive as I am in sports and academics. It's not that I don't have anything to say, it's just that I'm usually too shy to say it. Dad says I'll grow out of it once I go to college and get out in the world. He was the same way when he was younger, but seeing him now, you'd never know it. He's a brilliant businessman and the epitome of confidence.

Gunner cuts into the last bite of his chicken. "Maybe if the weather breaks, you and I can play a game. You can show me your moves." His crooked grin cuts the dimples into his cheeks.

My face blazes again. "Yeah, okay."

It's been bleak and drizzly for two days, and we're forecast to get sleet overnight, but we might reach sixty degrees in a few days. What can I say? December in North Carolina can be a meteorologist's nightmare. Freezing one day, warm enough for a T-shirt the next. If Gunner is serious about shooting hoops with me, there's a good chance the weather will cooperate at least once in the next three weeks while he's here.

Nick drops his napkin on his empty plate and pushes away from the table. "I'm out. I'm picking up Missy in thirty minutes. We're going to a movie."

Mom pouts in protest. "But you just got home."

He downs the rest of his iced tea and plunks the glass on the table. "Mom, I'll be home for three weeks. There'll be plenty of time for us to visit. Missy leaves for her grandparents' in a few days, so I want to spend some time with her."

Nick is super serious about Missy. It's just a matter of time before he pops the question, which my mom wants more than anything, so I can already tell she'll cave in three, two, one . . .

"Fine, honey," Mom says in surrender. She takes Nick's hand and squeezes it. "Just make sure you bring her by the house before she leaves so we can visit."

"I will." Nick bends and kisses her cheek then bolts up the stairs to get ready.

My mom rises and begins clearing the dishes. "Do you have any plans while you're back, Gunner?"

He sets his silverware on the plate and leans back. "Not really." He glances at me. "I haven't thought much about anything other than taking a break from school and getting some rest." He turns toward my dad then looks between him and my mom. "By the way, thank you for letting me stay here over the holiday."

His dad was sent overseas on business last week, and his mother went with him. According to Nick, they offered to fly Gunner over for the holiday, but he declined when Nick told him he was welcome to stay with us.

"Of course." My mom starts for the kitchen with her hands full of dishes. "That's better than spending the holiday alone, and I know we're all very happy to have you. Right, Cameron?" She shoots me a pointed smile, sending flames through my face again.

"Uh, yeah." I nod briskly, biting my lip.

Everyone helps clear the table, and I help my mom clean the kitchen while Gunner and my dad head off to look for a game on TV. Nick breezes through a few minutes later, grabbing a baggie of decorated cookies to give to Missy. After a quick kiss on Mom's cheek, he's out the door and probably won't be home until after midnight.

My mom sprays down the counter and begins wiping it off. "Gunner's grown into quite the attractive young man, hasn't he?" she says quietly.

I glance toward the living room. Gunner and my dad are talking football, so they're completely absorbed.

I meet my mom's eyes and catch the girlish giggle before it can leave my throat. "I can't believe he's going to be here for *three weeks*."

She starts the dishwasher. "Yeah, and three weeks will be gone before you know it, so scoot." She gestures for me to leave the kitchen. "Don't waste your time in here with me "

"I can't just go out there."

"Why not? This is your house. You can go wherever you want."

"You know what I mean."

She wipes her hands, grabs a clean plate from the cabinet, and then hands it to me. "Take them some cookies." She nods toward the full platter on the counter. "Go on."

I glance from Gunner to my mom and back again.

"Go, Cameron." She dips her head pointedly at the platter.

I take a deep breath, and with trembling hands, I arrange a variety of cookies on the plate, give my mom one last glance for courage, then head into the living room.

"Do you want some cookies?" I set the plate on the coffee table, eyes downcast, then take a seat on the far end of the couch as casually as I can.

I don't know why I'm suddenly so nervous around Gunner. He's been coming around for years. He's as much my friend as Nick's. It's just that I've always wanted him to be so much more.

But it's more than that. Something about Gunner is different. I felt it the moment our eyes met in my bathroom. Not only has his appearance changed, but something in his energy has changed, too. The air around him vibrates with a supercharged current that makes my heart beat harder.

"Thanks." He picks up one of the cookies and bites into it, giving me an appreciative wink that makes my insides somersault.

Three weeks.

With Gunner.

Maybe they won't last forever, but I'm sure going to try and make the most of them.

Chapter 3

My parents go to bed at eleven, leaving Gunner and me alone in the living room.

My mom's already warned me not to hover all over Gunner while he's staying with us, and she and my dad have cautioned against any "funny business" and said I should lock the bathroom door into Wendy's room, just in case. They needn't worry. Gunner hasn't shown any interest in me beyond checking me out in my towel. Still, I reassured them they raised a responsible daughter and that I would lock the door.

I'm not sure why they're so weirded out. I'm pretty sure they know I'm still a virgin, so I've given them no reason to think I'm that kind of girl.

Then again, this is Gunner. I would love to be that kind of girl with him.

He and I watch the last hour of *Prometheus* without uttering a single word to one another. The silence reminds me of those Halloween toys that are motion sensitive and move when you get close to them. It feels like at any moment, one of us is going to move and set off the other.

But that doesn't happen. The movie ends at midnight without incident, and after exchanging a couple of awkward glances with him, I push myself off the couch.

"I'm going to head up to bed."

"Yeah, me, too." He shuts off the TV.

On our way out of the living room, I turn off the lights, casting us into dimly lit darkness.

For a moment, neither of us moves, and I stare up at him in the silence. He's standing close to me. The house is so quiet, I can hear him breathe.

He starts up the stairs, and I follow.

"Don't trip," I tease, emboldened by the darkness.

"Will you catch me if I do?" he says over his shoulder. His voice rumbles over my senses.

"Uh, no. You might crush me."

"Are you saying I'm fat?"

I let out an abrupt laugh. "Gunner, trust me, you are *anything* but fat." I realize too late how that sounded. I don't want to scare Gunner away by revealing how I feel about him. "Um . . . what I mean is that you look like you've been working out."

He chuckles as we reach the top of the stairs. "I know what you meant."

My eyebrows tuck toward the inside corners of my eyes. "What do you mean?"

"Nothing. I'm just razzing you." Something in his tone indicates there's more to it than that, but he doesn't seem interested in explaining further.

He approaches Wendy's bedroom and pushes open the door.

Turns out that's where he'll be sleeping while he's staying with us, so we'll be neighbors. How's that for falling under a lucky star?

"Good night, Cami."

I stop at my bedroom door and glance back at him. "Night."

He hesitates, watching me, then turns and disappears inside Wendy's room.

Inside my own, I change into a pair of pink cotton shorts and a white tank top. I can't sleep in anything that covers my arms and legs, no matter how cold it is outside. I'll sleep under a dozen quilts before wearing long-sleeved, long-legged flannel pajamas like my dad does.

I brush my teeth and wash my face then shut my door to the bathroom in case Gunner wants to use it, but I think he's decided to use the one in the hall so we don't have any more near misses like the one this afternoon.

I turn on my TV and click through the channels for a while then shut it off when nothing catches my attention.

I try to read, but after going over the same sentence ten times and still not comprehending what it says, I give up and shut off my light. Closing my eyes, I give in to the fantasies of Gunner that have been calling to me all night.

I imagine myself going to his room, crawling into his bed, kissing him, him kissing me back. He takes off my pajamas, sucks my nipples, rolls me to my back and —

I hear a noise. A squeaky hinge. I know that sound. After years sharing a bathroom with Wendy, I know what it sounds like when her bathroom door opens.

Oops. I forgot to lock it as I promised.

I open my eyes and glance at my closed bathroom door. What's Gunner doing? Locked door or not, I thought he had decided to use the hall bathr —

The handle on my door turns, jarring me from my line of thought. Sucking in my breath, I quickly slam my eyes shut just as the door starts to open.

Exhilaration kicks me in the gut.

Why is Gunner coming to my room?

I'm instantly wide awake, but I keep my eyes closed.

His quiet footsteps cross the carpet, drawing closer to the bed.

I'm not imagining this, am I?

I don't dare open my eyes. Maybe he'll think I'm asleep and leave. Do I want him to leave? Not really. But do I really want him to stay?

The bed dips as he eases down on it, close to my feet.

Why is he in my room? What does he want?

I force myself to keep my eyes closed even though

I'm freaking out. But in a good way. Gunner has come to me. He's in my bedroom. He's on my bed. Probably watching me as I pretend to be asleep.

And now he's slowly pulling down the covers.

"I know you're awake," he says, his voice a low rumble, like thunder in the distance.

I don't respond. I remain absolutely still, even when he drags the covers all the way off my body. Even when his fingertips traipse up my bare shin to my knee. Even when he shifts closer, bends forward, and kisses the top of my thigh.

It's all I can do not to moan as electric tingles erupt from the contact between his lips and my skin, setting my insides on fire.

"Fine, pretend you're asleep." He makes a quiet noise, like a soft chuckle. "It's more fun that way."

I wouldn't know if it's more fun this way or any other. All I know is that I don't want him to stop touching me, kissing me, seducing me.

His fingers skim up and down my leg, and he leaves tender, full-lipped kisses on my thigh in a back-and-forth pattern that creeps higher, toward the hem of my shorts.

My body quickens, even as a voice inside my head—one of fear, because I've never done anything like this before—tells me to make him stop. But a louder voice tells me to let him keep going. Not to stop him. That this is what I've always wanted, and now I'm getting it. Gunner is touching me, kissing me, and, if I'm not mistaken, he's about to do naughty, delicious things to me that I've only read about in the books my mom doesn't know I read. The dirty books. The ones with the incredible sex scenes that get me wet between the legs and make me want to touch myself.

He shifts closer and places his hands on the waist of my shorts. I lock up even though I'm trying hard not to move.

He freezes. For a long moment, he doesn't do or say anything, then whispers, "If you want me to stop, tell me."

I don't.

He's still touching the waist of my shorts, but he doesn't move for a long time, as if he's watching me for a sign, making sure I'm okay with what's happening. Or maybe he's questioning whether I really am awake, as if perhaps he got it wrong and I really am asleep.

I can hear his accelerated breathing. Each deep inhale rushes down his windpipe, and each exhale sounds like a step closer to whatever he's planning to do to me.

The seconds tick by, neither of us showing our hand, both of us locked inside a moment that feels more like a fork in the road. If he stops, we go back to what we were before he walked through my door. Once more, he'll be the boy I've secretly been in love with and pined after for years, and I'll be his best friend's baby sister.

But if he continues and takes off my shorts, he'll become the first boy I've let see me naked, touch me sexually, and maybe even have an orgasm with if everything goes well. I'll be the young woman he desires.

Who knows what could happen and how far this could go? And that's what's so exciting about all this. It's different. We're becoming new people to one another. We're seeing each other in a fresh light with new possibilities blossoming between us.

He moves, making the mattress dip as he bends forward. When he speaks again, his voice comes from right beside my ear as he whispers, "If you don't tell me to stop right now, I'm going to take off your shorts, and I'm going to put my mouth on you, and I'm not going to stop until I've made you come."

Oh God. OhGodohGodohGodohGod . . .

"Last chance, Cameron. If you don't want this, tell me."

I still don't say anything.

"I won't do this unless I know you want me to. Do you want me to keep going?"

His head is still beside mine, his mouth beside my ear.

Drawing in a breath, I hold it for a moment then whisper, "Yes," so softly it could almost pass as a gentle breeze. For all he knows, I'm talking in my sleep.

But he knows I'm not. He knows this is the permission he's been seeking.

"Then get ready," he whispers back, before lightly kissing the spot right below my ear.

This is it. It's finally going to happen. Well, not *it*. He didn't say he was going to have sex with me. Just put his mouth on me. But that's still a really big *it*. I've never experienced oral sex. I've read about it. I've read hot sex scenes in those dirty books where the man does that to the woman. I've even masturbated while thinking of a man—Gunner—doing that to me. But I've never experienced it firsthand.

I don't make a sound. In fact, I'm practically holding my breath. I can't even move as I wait for what comes next.

My heart begins racing as I feel my shorts drag lower, past my hips, lower still, until I'm totally exposed. In the silence, I hear him swallow, and it sounds like he licks his lips or presses them together. I'm not sure.

The bed rocks gently as he continues dragging my shorts down my thighs. Then I feel warm air at the juncture between my legs just before his lips and nose brush through the fine dusting of blond hair down there.

I suck in a gulp of air and gasp. My whole body tenses as incredible sensations rocket through me.

That intimate caress does more to obliterate my sexual response than touching myself ever did.

Then his fingers part me, and his tongue lightly sweeps over my clit. If I thought my response to his lips and nose was off the charts, I nearly pass out from feeling his tongue. I arch off the mattress, and a high-pitched squeak breaks from my throat before I clamp it down. I don't want to wake up the whole house. That would put an end to my newfound relationship with Gunner before it ever starts.

Keeping his mouth on me, he finishes taking off my shorts and climbs between my legs, pushing my thighs wider as he settles on his stomach. His hands slide up my inner thighs, and he uses his thumbs to spread my lips as he closes his mouth over me.

Oh God!

I've had orgasms before. I know what it feels like when I'm approaching one. I know what it feels like to have one. What I'm experiencing right now is neither and both all at once. I feel like I'm already on the verge of coming while still feeling like I'm not even close. It's the most deliriously intense sensation I've ever experienced. I'm riding the edge of climax without going over. I want this feeling to last forever.

His mouth closes over my clit with gentle suction, and his tongue flicks slowly then fast then slow again. I like slow. I want slow. Slow feels better. Slow makes me hotter, and I roll my hips against his face, gasping as I feel the first spark of orgasm light inside me then flicker out to leave me skating on the razor's edge once more, which is fine by me. The longer I can make this last, the longer I can experience this explosive pleasure Gunner has awakened inside me.

His large hands grip my inner thighs, pushing my legs wider as he feasts on me, moaning, breathing against my wet flesh. Releasing my clit, he draws his tongue up the inside of one lip then down the other, over and over, making large, agonizingly electric circles that tease my clit at the top of each sweep, jolting me with growing urgency each time he makes contact.

Unbidden, my hips begin rocking against his mouth, and he groans low and deep as he pushes forward, hiking my legs over his shoulders at the knees as he scoops his hands under my bottom and pulls me more firmly against his mouth.

His tongue, his lips, his hot breath, the vibration that rumbles through my core every time he moans. I'm about to lose my mind with the need to come.

With my eyes still closed, my breath coming in short, almost panicked bursts, my head thrashes uncontrollably on my pillow as the sensations rise inside me. Somehow my hands find their way to his head, and my fingers drive into his hair, clenching down hard, gripping fistfuls of his thick, messy locks, making them even messier. His head rocks forward and back as his tongue lashes me, and then his mouth closes over my clit again, his tongue working in soft, tight circles that send me reeling.

"Ah!" My back arches as the telltale signs of

pending release surge through me.

I hold my breath. I go completely still. The pleasure crescendos.

Then everything goes white as I explode in a powerful rush, and I clamp my legs around Gunner's head, rocking my hips as every muscle in my body erupts.

Gunner's mouth stays on me, his tongue pressed hard against my clit but unmoving, as if he instinctively knows any more stimulation right now would be too much.

My body quakes and shudders, and then I collapse against the mattress, thoroughly blissed.

My eyes are still closed, and I'm breathing heavily, a smile on my face.

Gunner remains between my legs for a long time, his lips pliant, dropping soft kisses up and down my labia, against my still-sensitive clit, on my inner thighs.

I'm in heaven. Talk about Christmas wishes coming true! Of all the things I wanted for Christmas, I never imagined Gunner would become my favorite gift.

Minutes pass, neither of us moving or speaking. Just when I think he's fallen asleep between my thighs, he moves, gently lifting my legs off his shoulders. He eases off the bed without a word, tucks me under the covers, and then quietly tiptoes his way back to the bathroom.

Cracking my eyelids, I catch his retreating form just as he passes through the door, casts a quick glance back at me, and then closes the door behind him with a barely audible click of the latch.

Only then do I let out the heaviest sigh ever as I flop my arms to the sides and grin like a lovesick fool at my ceiling.

Gunner went down on me.

Gunner gave me an orgasm.

Gunner likes me.

Holy shit!

Chapter 4

I don't remember falling asleep, but I'm out of bed the moment I wake up. There's no time to waste after what happened last night. Everything's different between Gunner and me now.

Darting into my bathroom, I cringe at my reflection and the tangled mass of blond hair around my face. I quickly brush it out before jumping in the shower. I'm done in record time and change into a pair of jeans and a Highland Creek long-sleeved tee before drying my hair and heading downstairs for breakfast.

My mom is already in the kitchen whipping up pancakes. My dad is sitting at the table, reading the news on his iPad while sipping coffee. Gunner is texting someone. His eyes meet mine briefly before he turns his attention back to his phone.

Hmph. Okay then. That's not exactly the reaction I expected from him the morning after he licked me to Utopia.

"Good morning, honey," my mom says as I make my way to the fridge with a little less enthusiasm.

"Morning." I pull out the orange juice and pour a

glass.

"Did you see Nick come home last night?" she asks.

I shake my head while downing my juice. Apparently, sex makes a girl extra thirsty. I pour another glass. "He still wasn't home when Gunner and I went to bed."

Gunner's eyes shoot to mine, and I realize how what I said must have sounded. I feel like I just announced to the whole world that Gunner and I spent a lot of time in *my* bed last night. *Together.* Doing naughty things no one was supposed to know about.

But my mom is oblivious, cutting me off as I'm about to explain what I meant. "I'll let him sleep in a little longer then. I'm sure he's tired."

My mom doesn't even seem to mind that Nick was probably with Missy all night, and that they were probably having sex a dozen times. He may not have even come home. For all I know, he and Missy spent the night in a hotel. Not that I think her parents would let her do that, but she's a college student, too. Her mom and dad can't hold any illusions that she's still a virgin like I am. She and Nick have been together four years. They've been having sex for a while. I've heard them.

God, I hope no one heard me last night.

I slide the jug of orange juice back in the fridge then take a seat at the breakfast bar.

"I hope he doesn't sleep too late," Gunner says,

nonchalantly scrolling through his phone like today is just any other day. Like he didn't sneak into my bedroom, whisper dirty declarations into my ear about how he was going to put his mouth on me and make me come, and then followed through on his promise. "He's supposed to take me to my house this morning so I can get my mom's car."

I nibble my bottom lip then take a sip of my juice. Why would he need his mom's car? Is he planning on going somewhere? Does this mean he won't be staying with us, after all? What if he's decided he can't be here after what we did last night?

That would suck.

"Cami can take you," my mom says brightly. Too brightly.

A cold rush blasts through my body, followed by heat as my face warms.

"You wouldn't mind?" Gunner says, unaffected, like he never had his face between my legs or his mouth on my clit.

Maybe I dreamed the whole thing.

"Sure, I can take you. No biggie." If he can act like nothing happened, so can I. I turn away from him. "So, mom, how long on those pancakes? I'm starved."

* * *

An hour later, Nick is still in bed—and yes, he did come home last night, or, more like, in the wee hours of the morning—so Gunner folds himself into the passenger seat of the lava red Fiat 500 my parents bought me for my birthday last year. He looks comical with his long legs and torso crunched into the tiny space.

"Does this seat move back?" He searches for a lever or button to give him more leg room.

"Yeah, it's over there." I point, not daring to get any closer.

"Where?" He fumbles around.

"There."

"I'm not finding anything."

Giving in, I lean across his body, find the lever to adjust the seat, and then freeze when his hand brushes against mine.

Memories of those hands taking off my shorts and pushing against my thighs flood my brain, and I suck in my breath as I turn my gaze to his.

His eyes lock on mine, and his Adam's apple bobs up and down once as he searches my face. But he doesn't say a word. He reveals nothing of our tryst.

Clearing my throat, I pull away from him, start the engine, and try to get my head together. This is Gunner. Yes, last night was strange and thrilling and confusing, but he's still Gunner. I may have a crush on him, but he's still my friend. I can get through this.

"So, why do you need your mom's car?" I force myself to sound casual as I pull out of the driveway.

"Christmas shopping."

I throw him an incredulous look. "You haven't done your Christmas shopping, yet?"

"Hey, I've been busy studying. You try to get your shopping done during finals."

I laugh. "Excuses, excuses."

Now that I've concluded that last night was probably just a one-time thing and that Gunner wants to forget it happened, it's easier to fall back into friendly banter. Note that I didn't say it was *easy*, just easier, because yeah, I'm hurt. I wanted last night to mean more to Gunner. I wanted it to mean as much to him as it did to me. But if it doesn't, it doesn't. I can cry about that later. Right now, we're together. And that's good enough.

"You'll be in college next year," he says, "so you'll understand soon enough."

We ride in silence for a while.

"So," he says, "speaking of college, do you know where you're going, yet?"

I shrug. "I've sent out applications. My counselor told me my chances are good that I'll get into whatever school I want."

"Where did you apply?"

"North Carolina, Michigan, University of Florida."

"Florida?" He throws me an agitated glance like that's the last place he thinks I should go. "Why the University of Florida?"

"Duh. It's in Florida. Who doesn't want to go to

college where it's warm all year?"

He makes an irritated noise. "You don't pick a school based on what state it's in. You're supposed to go to the best school for what you want to study. Besides, it gets cold in Florida. It's a wet cold, too, so it's even worse than winters here. It's the kind of cold that cuts right through you." He glances out the window and clears his throat. "Do you know what you want to study?"

"Sports medicine."

"Really?" He brightens. "Ohio State has one of the best sports medicine programs in the country. You should apply there. You have until February. We could all be together again. Nick and I could show you around campus. It'll be fun."

I did apply to Ohio State, and if they accept me, I'm pretty sure that's where I'll go, but I'm kind of enjoying playing with him, especially since he seems determined not to talk about last night.

"I'll think about it."

I pull onto his street. Less than a minute later, I turn into his parents' driveway.

"Thanks for the ride." He unfolds himself from the passenger seat and climbs out.

"Any time."

He hesitates before shutting the door, bent at the waist so he can see inside the car. He's looking at me as if he wants to say something. He doesn't, though. After a few seconds, he drops his gaze.

"Thanks again." He stands.

"Have fun shopping," I call, wishing I were going with him. More than anything, though, I wish he'd say something about last night. I'm dying to know what he's thinking and whether that was a one-time deal, especially after his persuasive arguments to apply to OSU so "we can all be together again."

He waves over his shoulder and marches up the driveway to the house, his keys in his hand.

As I drive away, I'm more confused about my relationship with Gunner than I've ever been.

* * *

Gunner spends the whole day shopping and comes back to our house with a half-dozen shopping bags, which he takes directly to his room, where he stays until it's time for dinner.

Nick invited Missy over for dinner, so conversation focuses on her, where her family is going for the holiday, and how she's doing in her classes. Mom teases Nick like she always does about when we can expect an engagement announcement. Of course, Nick dodges the question the way *he* always does, with a chuckle and a remark about how Mom will just have to wait like everyone else.

Through it all, Gunner pointedly avoids looking at me. I'm beginning to think there's something wrong with him or me or both.

After dessert, my mom checks the time then pushes away from the table. "Okay, kids, your dad and I have to get ready for the company Christmas party."

"The first of *many* parties," my dad adds with an unenthusiastic sigh, standing reluctantly and tossing his napkin on his plate.

He's not much into parties and would rather stay home, but he says that some of the biggest business decisions all year get made at the holiday party, so he has to attend or risk missing out.

"I wonder who's going to get drunk this year," he says as he sets his plate and empty glass beside the sink.

My mom laughs. "Careful, Scott. That was you last year."

"Hey, I had to do something to get through the evening. If I had to listen to Walter tell one more knock-knock joke sober, I might have slit my own throat." He makes a face that conveys torture.

"It wasn't that bad." My mom starts putting the leftovers away.

"Says you." My dad turns to Nick and me. "You kids are on your own until morning, so don't burn down the house."

I perk up. "You're not coming home after the party?" This is an unexpected surprise.

My mom lets out a breathy giggle. "After what happened last year, we booked a room. That way your dad can drink if Walter starts telling jokes again, and I don't have to drive us home at two in the morning."

She's still fussing around in the kitchen when she should be following my dad upstairs to get ready.

As Nick, Gunner, and Missy drift off to the basement, I snag the dish of leftover potatoes from my mom. "I've got this, Mom. You don't need to be messing up your hair."

She had her hair done this afternoon and has been very careful all night not to destroy the stylist's work.

"You sure?"

I scoop the potatoes into a Tupperware container. "Yeah. Go get ready."

"Thanks, honey." She pats my hand then hurries up the stairs, leaving me to load the dishwasher and tidy up even as I hear the first clack of pool balls hitting each other downstairs.

As I stack the dirty dishes by the sink then wipe down the stove, my brain dives back into the land of daydreams. I've been living there a lot in the last twenty-four hours.

In my fantasy, this is my house. *Our* house. Gunner's and mine. Gunner and I live here together. We're married and have sex every day, rotating from room to room. Tonight, he comes to me in the kitchen, bends me over the counter, and . . .

The image in my head makes me blush.

My thoughts immediately turn toward what he did to me last night, and my insides transform into hot mush. Butterflies flutter to life in my belly as I remember how his tongue felt caressing my clit, flicking over it, teasing it. I'm practically panting as I rinse off another plate and set it in the dishwasher.

"Hey."

I jump and spin around as Gunner enters the kitchen, beelining for the fridge.

He stops and holds up his hands as he lets out a short laugh. "Whoa, sorry. I didn't mean to scare you."

Warmth invades my body at the sight of him. His full lips flatten into a straight line as he bites back a smile and opens the refrigerator.

"You startled me. My mind was . . ." It was obsessing over him, but I can't tell him that. I wave my soap-covered hand over the sink, dropping suds onto the stainless steel. "I was thinking about something."

He pulls out a two liter of Pepsi and shuts the door. "Sounds serious."

"School stuff," I lie.

He eyes the dirty dishes on the counter. "Need a hand in here?"

"No, that's okay. I've got it."

He starts out of the kitchen, flicking me a backward glance. "Join us downstairs when you're finished. We can play doubles. You and me against Nick and Missy." He winks. "We'll kick their asses."

How can I say no?

"Sure, okay. Give me a few minutes."

He disappears down the stairs.

Mom and Dad appear a short while later looking glamorous in a sequined dress and a tuxedo, and my dad is carrying an overnight bag.

"Good night, honey," my mom says, following my dad to the door. "Remember," she adds with a raised eyebrow, "behave yourself with Gunner."

My face heats. If only she knew.

"You're keeping the bathroom door locked, right?" she asks.

I give a tight nod as my mouth goes dry. "Of course."

She smiles. "Sorry if I'm being overprotective, Cami. It's just that I know you really like Gunner, and . . ." Her smile widens as she lowers her voice. "I think you might have finally caught his eye."

My heart skips a beat. "W-what makes you say that?" I swallow past the dryness in my throat.

She winks. "Women's intuition." She kisses my cheek. "He's been looking at you differently."

"Differently?"

She takes a step back. "Like he wants to ask you out."

My dad finally enters the conversation. "And you tell him I said you're not allowed to date until you're *thirty*." He's smiling, so I know he's kidding. He's always liked Gunner.

"Oh, honey" — my mom lightly swats his arm — "stop teasing."

"Who's teasing?" He knots his wool scarf around his neck.

My mom shakes her head and addresses me again. "Have a good time, honey. Just be the responsible daughter we know you are." She lets my dad direct her toward the door.

"Call if you need us for anything," he says.

I just want them to hurry out so I can breathe again. This whole conversation has hit too close to home, making my heart race.

"I will. Have fun," I call after them as the door to the garage closes.

It shuts with a finality that feels like relief and freedom.

I know it sounds crazy, because Nick and I have always been responsible kids. We'll never do something stupid like have a wild party or play with a Ouija board just because our parents are out for the night. But it doesn't change the atmosphere that comes with being parentless. The house is ours for at least twelve hours. We can play adult for a change. Nick has been adulting for a couple of years now that he's off at college, but for me, this is a rarity.

I finish up in the kitchen then go to my room to freshen up before joining the others in the basement.

I stop when I enter my bathroom. There's a white box with a gold and chiffon ribbon around it on the counter. An envelope is tucked under the ribbon.

Curious, I pull the envelope free and slide out the

small notecard inside.

Wear this to bed tonight. <u>Only</u> this.

That's it. No signature. No greeting. But I would recognize Gunner's neat handwriting anywhere.

He's avoided the topic of what we did last night all day. Now he's left me a gift. Something he wants me to wear to bed. Does this mean he plans on visiting me again tonight?

My heart leaps into my throat as I go wet between my legs. Looks like I won't be behaving tonight after all. Sorry, Mom, not sorry.

I untie the ribbon and lift the top off the shallow box. Inside is a cascade of pale-pink chiffon and lace that drapes like a silken veil as I lift it from the box by its satin spaghetti straps. A wide satin ribbon circles the empire waist, and pleats of chiffon fall in a swish of see-through fabric.

Gunner wants me to wear this? To bed? Tonight? With nothing on underneath it?

The hem will barely cover me below the waist.

I set the sexy nighty back in the box, and with goosebumps prickling my entire body, I practically skip down the stairs.

He's coming to me again tonight.

Chapter 5

Gunner and I do, in fact, kick Nick's and Missy's asses in pool — twice — thanks to Gunner's superb skills with a cue, and then we make popcorn and watch a movie in the theater room. I can't tell you a thing about what we're watching, though. I'm too busy thinking about that slinky pink swatch of material awaiting me in my bathroom.

Gunner has no idea I've seen his special gift, but knowing he'll be paying me a visit again changes the entire mood of the evening, and I'm overly eager to go to bed.

As soon as the credits begin rolling on the screen, I stand and stretch, making a show of how tired I am.

"I'm beat," I say. "I'm heading up."

"Yeah, me, too." Gunner stands and yawns, but I can tell he's faking.

Nick and Missy appear oblivious but grateful for the privacy we're about to give them.

"'Night, guys," Nick calls as I lead Gunner out of the theater.

"'Night."

Gunner and I climb the stairs in silence. On the main level, I switch off the lights, and then we make our way to the second level. At the top of the stairs, we turn down the hall the same way we did last night. As I reach my door, I stop and glance over my shoulder as he does the same outside Wendy's bedroom door.

"Well . . . good night," I say.

"Good night." He remains still, watching me. A moment later, he pushes through the door, but not before I catch the hint of a smile cross his lips.

The moment his door closes, I rush into my bedroom and race to the bathroom. I wash my face, brush my teeth, apply lip gloss, spritz the nape of my neck with half a pump of baby powder-scented body mist, and grab the pale-pink nighty.

Returning to my room, I strip out of my clothes and put on the nighty. Pale pink has always been a good color on me, with my fair coloring and blond hair.

The fabric in the bust is stretchy, so while I don't fill it like a Victoria's Secret model, my breasts do feel snug within the bodice. As expected, the hem hangs just past the bottom of my panties, barely concealing me below the waist.

Speaking of panties, the note said that I was only to be wearing the nighty.

Turning away from my full-length mirror, I gingerly hook my thumbs in the elastic waist and push them down my legs, then step out of them.

I'm ready.

I think.

At least, I'm physically ready. Mentally is a whole other thing. I'm not sure I'll ever be mentally ready to welcome Gunner into my bed.

Whether I'm ready or not, it's going to happen, so I'd better prepare myself.

Pulling back the blankets, I climb into bed and turn off the light on my nightstand.

Will he come in right away? Will he make me wait? This is his game. All I can do is play along.

I'm a tense, nervous wreck, my fingers laced over my stomach, my legs straight and pressed together.

I look like a corpse on display at a funeral.

Loosen up, Cameron.

Taking a deep breath, I separate my hands and bend my legs, angling myself so I'm lying partially on my side, facing the door to the bathroom, of course.

Within seconds, I hear the door to Wendy's room open with its telltale squeak. I slam my eyelids shut and hold my breath. The door to my room opens, and his footsteps approach my bed. A moment later, my mattress dips as he sits down beside me.

"Are you going to pretend to be asleep again tonight?" he asks. I hear the smile in his voice.

I keep my eyes closed a moment longer then open them as I exhale. "No." I give him a resigned smile.

"Don't get me wrong" — his fingertips slide up my

arm, leaving tingling sparks in their wake — "I liked our game last night, but I think I'd like to see your eyes tonight."

"It's too dark to see my eyes."

"I can see them just fine."

"You can?"

"They're sparkling from the light coming in through the window."

"Oh." I sit up.

The blankets fall away, revealing the bodice of my nighty. His face is only a couple of feet from mine.

"Do you like it?" His gaze takes in the nighty as he lightly caresses my shoulder with his fingertips.

Tiny explosions blast through my body from the subtle caress, and my breath comes in more rapid, shallow bursts.

"Yes," I say shyly, dipping my head, hiding my face as I draw my legs up and wrap my arms around them.

"Nervous?"

I nod. "Yes," I whisper.

"Why?"

I shrug. I'm suddenly the quiet, mousy girl I was the first time I saw him six years ago. I don't know how to behave around him, anymore. We're no longer just friends, but we're not a couple, either. As far as I know, no one but us knows we've even hooked up, and it's probably a good idea we keep it that way. I doubt Nick would get upset, but it could make their friendship weird, and I know it would make my relationship with him awkward.

In a lot of ways, I'm seeing Gunner for the first time again. Once more, we're finding our way with one another.

He scoots closer, extending his arm over my legs to rest his hand on the mattress beside my hip. "After what we did last night, you're still shy?"

I nod and tuck my face more deeply toward my chest.

He dips his nose into my hair and whispers, "You're adorable when you're shy, Cameron, but I don't want you shy. I want you telling me how you want it so I can give it to you."

I lift my wide-eyed gaze to his. "What if I don't know how I want it?"

The corners of his mouth turn up, and his eyes narrow as if he just proved something he already knew. "You're still a virgin, aren't you?"

Heat blasts into my face, and I bite my lip. "Is it bad if I am?" I don't want him to change his mind and leave just because I've never had sex.

He shakes his head and catches my chin between his thumb and forefinger, preventing me from looking away. "No. That's not bad at all."

"But I've never done this before. I don't know what I want." I want *him*, but I know that's not what he's asking. He wants details. Hard or soft? Fast or slow? Do I like my breasts played with or not? And about a million other questions I don't have the answers to.

His lips brush over my cheek as he slides his mouth up to my ear. "Then I guess I'll have to help you figure that out," he whispers.

Feverish waves wash through me as he eases me back on the bed and takes off his shirt, leaving him in only a pair of nylon athletic shorts. He pulls back the covers and slides into bed beside me. For the longest time, he remains propped on his elbow, gazing into my eyes, running his fingertips up and down my arms, creating a pleasant sensation that slowly relaxes me.

"That feels good." I smile up at him.

He smiles back. "That's a start."

His fingers glide over my bare shoulders, back and forth over my collarbones. With each pass, his hand drops a little lower, toward my chest. Toward the boundary between my skin and the sheer nighty. I watch his face. His gaze follows his fingers, crawling lower. Heat blooms low in my belly, and my breathing accelerates.

When the tips of his fingers skim along the top of the fabric, I shiver.

"Do you like this, too?" He does it again.

"Y-yes."

"What about this?" His fingers sweep lower, making a circle around my nipple.

I inhale sharply and arch into his touch as tiny

explosions fan out from my breast.

He chuckles darkly. "I take that as a yes."

All I can do is nod. And pant. I'm definitely panting. I might even have moaned a little.

His hand glides over my breasts, teasing my nipples into erect nubs. All the while, his gaze travels over my body as if he's seeing me with fresh eyes.

He continues touching me, caressing me. We don't speak. Aside from our heavy breaths and occasional soft moans, we don't make a sound. But the more he touches me, the more of him I want. I want his hands all over my body. I want his mouth on me again, the way it was on me last night. I want to feel him. All of him.

Staring at the shadows playing over his muscled arm in the darkness, I lick my lips and tentatively reach out.

He stops and brings his gaze to mine just as my palm closes over his forearm. He feels solid and warm, strong, and I slowly trail my hand over his elbow to his biceps. His muscles flinch under my fingers as if my touch elicits a reflexive response.

I've never touched Gunner like this. So intimately. He's smooth and hard. Like steel wrapped in suede.

I blink my gaze to his and bite my bottom lip at the hungry way he's staring at me.

"I like touching you." I flatten my palm against his firm chest and feel it swell as he inhales.

He places his hand over mine, bends forward, and

brushes his lips over my mouth. "I like it when you touch me."

My lips simmer from his kiss, and I give him a faint nod, eager to do anything he asks.

He searches my face as if seeking permission. Whatever he finds in my expression must grant it, because a moment later, he gently eases himself on top of me. My legs naturally part so he can settle into the cradle of my body.

That's when I notice the tattoo on his chest and shoulder. In the darkness, it's hard to see, and I can't tell what it is, but—a tattoo! How dangerous! How atypical of him! Just the thought of quiet, mild-manner Gunner with a tattoo is enough to send a thrill through my girly parts.

"When did you get a tattoo?" I run the tips of my fingers over the shadowy pattern.

"In October."

I peer closer but still can't make out what it is. "What is it?"

He only smirks. "I'll show you later." He licks his lips. "Right now . . ." He dips down and presses a sensuous, full-lipped kiss against the swell of my breast, shutting off all thoughts of his tattoo. "My mind's on other things."

Mine suddenly is, too.

His fingers glide up the outside of my thigh to my hip. He looks up at me, and one of his eyebrows ticks upward. "You're not wearing any panties."

My skin sizzles as his palm settles around my hip, his fingers sinking into the flesh of my bottom as he squeezes. Hummingbirds take flight in my stomach.

I can barely find my voice to reply. "Your note said not to."

"I know, but I wasn't sure you'd go through with it."

"I wasn't, either."

"But you did." His fingers swish side to side on my bare hip. "So, what shall I do to you?" His voice rumbles ponderously.

I still can't believe this is happening, but I can't bring myself to question his motives right now. I just want more of what we did last night, more of his touch, more of him on top of me.

And since I've never done any of this before, I'm no help. Even if I *had* done this before, I'm so tongue-tied and twisted by the shock that he's actually in my bed that I couldn't vocalize what I want even if I knew.

He holds his body up on one elbow and plays with the spaghetti strap over my shoulder. "I guess I'll just have to keep making my way around your body and find out what else you like."

I nod, unsure of what else to do while under the intoxicating influence of this getting-sexier-by-the-second man I've always wanted but never thought I would have. I hoped, but I never dreamed anything like this would happen, especially when he never showed any interest in me. Or did he, and I just never noticed it?

He gently tugs the elastic bodice away from my left breast, but stops before revealing my nipple. "Is this okay?"

Unable to speak, I nod.

He nudges the fabric lower, and I hold my breath. And still lower, until with one final tug, he exposes my nipple at the same moment I expel the breath I'd been holding.

Goosebumps burst all over my body, making me shiver. The only people who've seen me naked are my parents when I was a little girl, and the girls in my gym class.

As his mouth closes around my puckered nipple, my eyes roll back. I close them, issuing a long moan as heat erupts through my back and shoulders, sweeping down through my stomach to jolt me between the legs.

"Do you like this?" he says softly, before flicking his tongue back and forth.

I lick my lips and open my eyes, glancing down to see his mouth engulf my nipple once more. With a shudder, I inhale then whisper, "Yes," as I exhale.

He grins and pulls down the fabric over my right breast, shifting his weight so his mouth hovers directly over my right nipple. "And this . . .?" His lips close and draw my flesh over his tongue.

I shudder and nod. "Uh-huh."

Gunner sure knows what he's doing. It's obvious

he's done this before.

I'm not sure how I feel about that. On one hand, I'm happy he comes skilled. If he didn't know what he was doing as much as I don't, this experience would be something else entirely.

On the other hand, the fact that he knows how to please a woman means he's done this with other girls.

How many others have felt his mouth on them like this? How many girls has he been with to give him his mastery over my body? He obviously knows what girls like and how to get them hot, but just how experienced is he?

He leaves a trail of kisses up my chest, and I tip my head back as he nibbles the side of my neck.

"And this? Do you like this, too?" His lips caress my neck, right below my ear. Then the tip of his tongue sweeps down to my collarbone.

I like everything he's doing to me. My God, I'm practically floating, it's so good.

"Y-yes."

He nips a simmering trail up the other side of my neck then closes his lips over my skin.

I'm nodding, moaning, panting. "I like when you do that," I whisper, closing my eyes again and squirming under him, bending my legs, involuntarily rocking my hips as need and arousal spear the heart of me.

He groans and rolls his body in a long, luxurious wave as he brings his mouth to mine and draws my bottom lip between his teeth on a growl. At least it sounds like a growl. Whatever it was, I like it. It's hot. It's the sound I imagine a man makes when he wants something badly enough to let his inner caveman come through. The kind of sound that says he likes what I'm doing, too.

Following his lead, I bite his bottom lip, sucking it into my mouth the way he did mine, the student taking a note from the teacher. He moans again, sinking against me, rolling his hips, his hardness pressing right where it makes me feel good.

Without my panties, all that's between us is the thin, slippery nylon of his shorts, and the friction his body creates with mine is the kind that I create with my finger when I want to make myself come, only better.

I gasp, locking my arms around him, lifting my hips to increase the pressure.

The dark, silky moan that escapes his throat is one of surprise and approval. "Do you like that?" he whispers against my mouth.

I nod, my gaze locked to his, boldness replacing timidity. With each passing moment, my body's needs take over, kicking my shyness and fear into the shadows. All that's left is wanton desire. Lust. Hunger. The need to come and release all this pent-up energy coiling within my belly.

He rocks against me again, sending shards of fire and ice through my body. "Can you come like this?"

I nod eagerly, wrapping my legs around his, grinding myself against him. I've masturbated enough to know the kind of friction I need to get off. If we keep moving against one another this way, it's only a matter of time before I explode. An orgasm is already budding inside me.

"Then come for me," he says forcefully. "Let me feel it. Let me see it."

As his mouth crashes over mine, he grabs my arms and thrusts them to the mattress before shoving them over my head, pushing my pillow against the headboard. His body rolls and rocks against mine, but he keeps the pressure between my legs, his hardness rubbing against me in the most perfect way as his mouth assaults mine.

This is so much better than my finger. So much better than masturbation. We're all tongues, lips, mouths, and fire, moving against one another like we're having sex, the only thing between us a thin layer of nylon.

"Tell me when you're close," he growls before driving his tongue into my mouth.

He's overwhelming my senses. His energy is heat and lava and surging ocean waves.

"I'm close," I murmur, straining against the hold he has on my wrists.

God, he's good. This is better than I thought it could be. I never imagined being with him could be like this.

His grip loosens on my arms as he surges forward and back, stimulating my clit as the sensations rise inside me. Sensations that let me know I'm about to fall over the edge. Will he catch me?

"Hold me as you come," he murmurs against my teeth.

I'm almost there. So close. Every part of me tightens as I rock my hips with increased urgency, needing just a little . . . bit . . . more.

"Ah!" I fling my arms around him, arching off the mattress as I crest.

His mouth smashes against mine, and he's drinking in all of me as I gasp and cry out, shuddering and quaking beneath him as my climax plows into me.

I've never felt anything like this. Ever!

It's like I've flown into heaven. For a few brief seconds, I know what it's like to die and pass through the pearly gates. Then I'm back inside my body again, my arms and legs clamped so tightly around him that it's a wonder he can breathe.

I unravel myself, and he quickly rolls to the side.

"Give me your hand," he says in a rush, snatching it as he shoves down the waist of his shorts.

He's so big! Then again, I have nothing and no one to compare him to.

Before I have much of a chance to admire the hard length that just sent me to the moon, he places my hand on his cock then wraps his hand around mine. Our fingers intertwine as he guides me to stroke him fast and hard.

"Jesus!" He slams the back of his head against the pillow then looks at me. "Kiss me."

I push toward him, finding his mouth with mine as he jacks our joined hands up and down his erection.

He's tense and breathing hard, sucking in huge gulps of air through his nose as his lips devour mine, his tongue diving into my mouth.

I feel him grow harder beneath my palm as he seems to swell even more, and then he breaks our kiss.

"Oh, God, Cami, I'm coming!"

For a split second, everything goes still. His hand, his body, his very soul, and then he grunts hard as his erection jerks in my hand. His eyes lock to mine then close as his head falls back, and his whole body pulses as a stream of semen shoots out and lands on his washboard stomach, which twitches with each kick of his erection as he continues working my hand up and down his shaft in punctuated strokes.

It's the most incredible, sexiest thing I've ever witnessed. And I did it. I helped. My hand was on him when he came. It was my mouth kissing his, my eyes he looked into, my name he cried out.

We did this together. We came as one. Both of us. He helped me reach release, and I helped him.

This is the single most glorious moment in my life. Gunner wants me as much as I want him.

He sighs and swallows, his glazed eyes still on mine. Licking his lips, he reaches around with his left hand. The hand that put a death grip on my comforter while he helped me stroke him with the other. He wordlessly brushes the hair off my face as if his thoughts are too scrambled to speak.

For the longest time, he just stares at me, caressing my face. Our joined hands are still wrapped around his cock, but it's softening.

The excitement over.

"Cameron?" He speaks my name as if he's addressing a princess.

"Yes?"

He cups my cheek. When he speaks again, his voice is dark and serious, almost foreboding, as if he's giving me a warning. "What we just did . . .?"

I hold my breath. Oh God, is he going to tell me we can never do it again? I don't think I could handle that.

His gaze locks expectantly to mine. "Before I go back to Ohio State, we're going to do that again. And when we do, I'm going to be inside you."

My mouth falls open, but I have no words to speak.

I was wrong. The excitement isn't over. It's just beginning.

Chapter 6

For the next week, Gunner and I fall into a pattern. I've got finals before my Christmas break starts, so I'm at school during the day, but when I'm not, Gunner and I act like nothing is going on between us. Some days he barely even talks to me, even when he helps me study for my calculus exam. He was always a math wiz.

But while the days reveal nothing of the growing intimacy between us, the nights are ours. He comes to my bed every night, and each time he does, he takes things a little bit further.

The first night, he goes down on me again, inserting a finger. I've done that before, but when he does, it feels different. Better. And I come the hardest yet as he finds the special place inside me that always makes my orgasms more intense.

The second night, he walks me through my first blow job. He seems impressed with my novice skills, which emboldens me to take him in my mouth again on the third night, when I experience my first sixty-nine.

On the fourth night, he pulls me on top of him. He's completely naked and I'm wearing only my panties, and we go through the motions of having sex again. He lets me come first then flips me onto my back and masturbates onto my stomach.

Feeling his fluid shoot all over my skin, so hot and sticky, makes me feel like he's marking me as his. I belong to him now.

I've never looked forward to going to bed as much as I have since Gunner started visiting my room every night. And with my parents attending parties and holiday dinners almost every evening, we have ample opportunity to spend time together.

The weekend before Christmas, I get a text from my best friend, Julie.

Christmas party at the Walkers' house tonight. You in?

Brenna and Zane Walker's parents live in a humongous mansion about ten minutes from my house. Brenna is my age, but Zane is the same age as Nick and Gunner, and they were pretty good friends in high school. No doubt Gunner will be at the party, too. When the Walker kids host a party, it's epic, and everyone attends.

I type out a reply.

Sounds fun. See you there.

It will be even more fun if Gunner goes.

I haven't told Julie about Gunner, yet. Something about what he and I are doing feels too special—too secret—to blurt even to my best friend, as if the moment I tell anyone what we've done, the magic bubble will burst, and it will all be over. I don't want it to be over, so the only people who know what he and I are doing are us.

Mom and Dad have yet another holiday party to go to tonight, and it's another all-nighter, so as Nick, Gunner, and I head out, they tell us to have a good time and that they'll see us in the morning.

Nick drives, and Gunner sits in the back while I take the passenger seat up front. I feel his eyes on me the whole time.

My phone vibrates with a text, and I pull it out of my pocket. The message is from Gunner.

You look nice tonight. Got a hot date?

I bite my bottom lip and fight the urge to giggle as I type out a reply.

Only if you feel like going public.

Part of me would love to walk in on Gunner's arm. All the other girls would be so jealous. But another part of me enjoys our secret rendezvous too much. It turns me on to think we'll be at this party, pretending we're not together, when he'll be in my bed later tonight when we get home.

Maybe tonight will be the night.

All these years, I've been saving my V-card for Gunner. Other boys have caught my eye from time to time, but not like Gunner. Not enough for me to consider giving my virginity to them.

Gunner promised by the time he leaves to go back to Ohio State, we'll have crossed that threshold. Which means that sometime between now and the day after New Year's, we'll have sex.

It's surreal to think about. Being with him has been a fantasy of mine for so long that the reality taking place between us doesn't feel entirely real. Every night when he comes to my room, I know he's there, but it feels more like a dream. One he confirms every morning when he hardly says anything to me during breakfast. But then he shows up again the next night, and the dream is real once more.

We arrive at the party and the three of us wander in together before splitting up. I gaze after Gunner as he strolls alongside my brother, waving at a couple of old friends on the other side of the room.

A pang of loss and confusion settles into my heart. Looks like the part of me who hoped to be "his girl" tonight is stronger than I thought, because seeing him high-five his old bros and exchange hugs with Mindy Talbot and Stacia Stevens, two of the most popular seniors at Highland Creek, feels like green sludge in the pit of my stomach.

Mindy and Stacia are all flirty smiles and starry eyes, and it's obvious both want a piece of Gunner.

Maybe they want to take a piece of him together. A threesome. I heard that they did that with another boy, and I thought for sure it would kill their reputation. It didn't. Somehow the rumor made them even more popular. Girls want to *be* them, and boys want to be *with* them. *All* the boys.

I'm sure their promiscuity will catch up to them someday, but, for now, they're riding a wave of popularity I can't compete with. I can't even imagine having a threesome. Mindy and Stacia are in a whole other league from me. A more grown-up league. A league more Gunner's speed.

Biting back my jealousy and sudden insecurity, I grab a beer from a large bucket of ice and go in search of Julie.

I don't normally drink at these parties. Not because I'm not old enough to drink, but because my parents raised me better than that. And because, unlike most of the people at the party, I don't really like alcohol. But I need to take the bitter edge off seeing Gunner with Mindy and Stacia, as well as all the biting images of them together rolling through my mind.

The house is packed. The Walkers have a huge home, but there's got to be three hundred kids here, and a couple of the smaller rooms have such tight quarters it's like squeezing a lemon through a straw to pass to the other side.

I finally find Julie in the room we all call the ballroom, even though that's not what it is. It's big enough to be one, though.

The vaulted ceilings form a seam over the center of the room, from which three chandeliers hang at precise intervals. They're made of shimmering clear glass balls of various sizes that look like Christmas bulbs. Each bulb has a small light inside, some are red while others are green, and the glass balls form an upside-down Christmas tree shape. Very festive.

The rest of the lighting in the ballroom is low, and music blares from speakers on either side of a DJ booth at the front of the room. I find Julie dancing with a group of our friends.

"Cameron!" She rushes forward to hug me. "Aren't the chandeliers awesome!" She looks up at the one directly over us.

"Yeah sure." I still haven't recovered from seeing Gunner with Mindy and Stacia even though I've already killed my beer and it's mellowed me out.

Julie frowns. "What's wrong?" The music is so loud she has to yell for me to hear her.

"Nothing." I force a smile, but Julie isn't buying it.

"Okay, you're talking to me right now." She drags me toward a group of tables set up around the makeshift dance floor.

I plop down across from her. "Julie, come on . . ."

"Is this about Gunner?"

I gape at her. I told her Gunner would be staying at my house over Christmas, but can she tell there's more? "Why would it be about Gunner?" I try to sound innocent.

"Duh, Cam. You've crushed on the guy since sixth grade. Everything is about Gunner."

My shoulders collapse, and I melt into my chair. "He's talking to Mindy and Stacia."

"What?" Julie gives me her I'll-slap-a-bitch look. "Those skanks. You're so much better than they are, Cam."

"I know, but—"

"No. No buts. If Gunner wants that trash, you don't need him. You just wipe him from your mind right now and look for someone else, because any guy who thinks Mindy and Stacia are better than you needs to get lost."

Julie makes it sound so simple. If only she knew how I've been spending my nights for the past week, she'd know things aren't as easy as they seem. Maybe I need to tell her. Not everything, of course, because that would take away too much of the magic. But maybe I could tell her just a little.

I sit forward. "He kissed me."

Julie blinks as if she has no idea what I just said, and then her eyebrows pop high into her forehead. "Who? Gunner?"

"Well, yeah. That's who we're talking about,

right?" I duck my head and tuck my hair behind my ear.

Her mouth falls open and she makes an I'm-so-happy-for-you sound. She goes hot and cold faster than a broken faucet. "Cameron, oh my God, when? How?"

Wanting to keep the good stuff to myself at least until he leaves, I blather out a story about how he was helping me study for finals one night then just leaned over and kissed me. That's sort of true. He did help me study. And he has kissed me.

She swats my arm. "I can't believe you didn't tell me!"

I shrug. "I didn't want to make more out of it than it was."

And now that I've seen how dangerous it is to get involved with him — because I'm always going to have to deal with girls like Mindy and Stacia fawning all over him — not making more out of what he and I are doing is critical. I need to do a better job of guarding my heart or he'll squash it.

"So he kissed you?" Julie bobs her eyebrows up and down. "Did you do anything else?"

"Nothing I want to talk about." I'm regretting saying anything, because I hate leaving Julie hanging, but I also just don't want to go into the details. At least not tonight.

"Oh come on, Cam, I'm your best friend. Tell me."

"I promise I will, but not right now, okay? Later.

After he goes back to Ohio."

Julie growls in frustration. "You're killing me here."

"I know. I'm sorry. Let's just dance and have a good time." I grab her hand and drag her back to the dance floor as the song changes to a dance mix of Selena Gomez's "Kill Em With Kindness."

Poignant, given where my mental state has taken me. Not that Gunner is lying to me, but he's not exactly making me feel secure in our relationship either.

Can I even call what we're doing a relationship? He's not my boyfriend. No one even knows we're messing around with each other. As far as the universe is concerned, we're just fuck buddies. And if we're fuck buddies, doesn't that mean he has the right to hook up with whoever he wants? For that matter, doesn't it mean I do, too?

These feelings and emotions are new to me, and I don't know what to make of them. I don't want to hook up with anyone else. Just Gunner. And we haven't even hooked up. Not technically. I'm still holding my V-card. He said he's going to take it before he leaves, but now I'm not sure. What if he's changed his mind? Mindy and Stacia might have him upstairs in one of the bedrooms right now, showing him how much he doesn't need me or my V-card.

The smart thing for me to do would be to just go home and forget everything. Lock myself in my bedroom and not come out until Christmas. I could get away with that now that I'm on break from school.

Before I can give the idea more serious consideration, I spin and catch Nick and Gunner entering the ballroom. Mindy and Stacia are nowhere to be seen, but a new complication has arisen. Simone Bradley. Gunner's ex-girlfriend. They dated his senior year at Highland Creek. They graduated together, but she ended up going to North Carolina instead of Ohio State. They broke up before graduation.

But that doesn't mean they won't get back together.

His gaze connects with mine, and I turn away, pulling Julie farther into the mass of dancing bodies. The last thing I want is a front-row seat to the resurrection of his and Simone's relationship.

For me, dancing is a release, and I let the bass-heavy rhythms swallow me. A new song spins into the mix, and I get lost in the music. It's safe there. Safe where I don't have to remember Gunner with Simone or Mindy or Stacia. It's just Julie and me, and I dance and laugh with her, letting myself go. Sweat trickles down my back, and my long hair sticks to my face and neck, but I don't stop.

Dancing is my third love behind basketball and band. Same with Julie. If not for basketball, we'd have joined the dance team. But the practice schedules conflicted, so we were forced to pick one or the other. It was a hard decision, but we decided on basketball.

Even so, we've been known to break into an impromptu dance routine on occasion. In fact, we're known for it at these parties, and we've spent hours choreographing our moves and learning dance routines from music videos.

When the music changes again and Missy Elliott's "WTF" kicks in, everyone around Julie and me lets out a cheer and pushes back to give us room. Julie and I threw down a routine to this song at the Walkers' end-of-summer party a few months ago, right before school started. Someone caught it on video, and within the first week of classes, everyone at school had seen it. The coaches for the dance team and cheerleaders even asked us to teach them the choreography so they could perform it at the homecoming pep rally.

In other words, it's a pretty epic routine.

Within seconds, the crowd has opened a large circle around us and half the cheerleaders and several members of the dance team have joined us and are already picking up with the choreography. Julie and I exchange glances and shrug as we join them, taking our places up front.

The crowd pulses with energy, surging and cheering. Some try to catch onto the steps.

And who should be standing right in front, his eyes glued to me?

Gunner.

Mindy and Stacia have reappeared by his side and

look irritated that our performance interrupted their attempts at getting his attention. Simone is still nearby, too, but I can't tell if she's trying to get his attention or not.

When the song finally ends to a round of shouts for an encore, I'm out of breath, coated with sweat, and in need of major thirst-quenching.

Escaping to the room's periphery, I find a bottle of water and down half of it as the crowd settles back down.

"That was awesome!" Julie says, crashing up behind me, snatching the bottle of water from my hand and downing the rest.

"Hey! That's mine!"

"Want it back?" Julie pretends she's going to stick her finger down her throat.

I hold up my hands. "Ew. No thanks." I grab another bottle off the bar behind me.

As I open the new bottle, I glance toward where Gunner had been standing. He's gone. So is his fan club. They're obviously tittering off after him now that the show is over.

Julie and I accept high fives and fist bumps from a few more of our fans, and then we go back to dancing. Gunner is nowhere to be seen. After a while, Julie grabs my wrist and gestures toward the back of the room.

"I have to pee," she shouts over the music.

I nod and follow her away from the undulating

throng.

Outside the ballroom, the party is in full swing, and from the tight quarters, it feels like at least a hundred more people have arrived since I got here.

"Shit, the line for the bathroom is going to be long," she says, tugging me along behind her.

"Luckily, there's about ten bathrooms in this house," I remind her.

"Yeah, and I bet they all have lines." We start up the spiral staircase in hopes that we'll have better luck away from the main crowd.

The upstairs isn't quite as packed as the lower level, but there's still a wait for the hall bathroom.

I stand beside Julie, and she squirms, shifting her weight from foot to foot.

"Nice moves downstairs." A couple of guys give us thumbs-up as they approach.

Looks like our epic dance routine is making the rounds again. Someone must have recorded it on their phone and e-mail blasted it to everybody.

"Thanks," I say, gazing after them as they pass.

I see a flash of red as a door opens down the hall. It's the same shade of red as Gunner's shirt. My view is temporarily blocked by a trio of laughing girls, and then they move to one side.

My heart drops. Gunner is coming out of what looks like a bedroom, and Simone is with him. She's straightening her blouse. They're smiling and talking animatedly, totally engaged with each other. So engaged that he doesn't even notice me staring painfully at him.

"What is it?" Julie asks as we inch closer to the bathroom. "What's wrong?" She follows my gaze then sucks in her breath as she turns back to me. "Oh, Cam, I'm sorry."

What just happened? Are Simone and Gunner back together? Did they just have sex? An empty ache settles in the floor of my chest. I'm not sure how I'm supposed to feel. Gunner and I weren't a couple or anything, but it felt like we were heading that way.

I creep back to hide behind Julie as I peer at him. He closes the bedroom door then follows Simone toward the stairs at the other end of the hall.

"Are you okay?" Julie asks, taking my hand.

My heart drops as I lean against the wall. I swear if the thing weren't there I would fall over. My legs don't feel like they can hold me up on their own right now.

"No," I say honestly. Why lie? Julie will just know I'm fronting.

"Maybe nothing happened."

"They were coming out of a bedroom," I remind her. "She was straightening her shirt."

"I know, but . . ."

"Yeah . . . but nothing." I drop my face into my hand. "I'm such an idiot."

To think I had a chance with him.

"You're not an idiot."

We move up another place in line.

"Just a fool then."

"You're not an idiot *or* a fool, Cam." She stands quietly for a moment. As we move into the spot at the head of the line, she squeezes my hand. "Do you want to go home?"

The night started out so well, but it's been nothing but an emotional roller coaster since walking through the door. I don't want to be here if I'm going to have to watch Simone climb all over Gunner and vice versa.

I sigh and nod, meeting Julie's eyes as the bathroom door opens. "Yeah."

She darts forward then turns back to me. "Give me a minute, and I'll take you. Just . . ." She flutters her hand and bounces on the balls of her feet like she's about to burst. "I'll be right back."

She quickly shuts the door, and I'm left in the hall to wait for her.

Alone.

That word just became my least favorite word in the whole world, because I have a feeling I'll be in my bed alone tonight for the first time since Gunner got back.

Chapter 7

"Text me if you need me," Julie says, dropping me off at home.

I wave as she drives away then head inside.

I break into sobs the moment the door closes behind me.

It feels like a hole has opened in my chest and my heart is trying to break free to leap to its death like a suicide jumper off the top of the Empire State Building.

Sniffling and wiping tears from my eyes, I trudge up the stairs to my bedroom.

The house is quiet. Mom and Dad won't be back until morning. Nick and Gunner might be out several more hours. And I'm going to my room to cry myself to sleep.

In my bathroom, I set my phone on the white marble counter and can't help checking it for messages.

Nothing. No text from Gunner.

Splendid.

He's probably with Simone.

In my reflection, my mascara is a tear-smudged mess, my eyes are bloodshot, and my face is blotchy. I'm an ugly crier. Just like my mom.

Nothing a little makeup remover can't fix.

I wash my face, take a shower to wash off all the dried sweat and bad memories of the evening, pull on a pair of shorts and a T-shirt, climb into bed, and turn on the TV.

I don't care what's on. I just need noise. Anything to help drown out the buzz of painful, insecure thoughts shooting through my mind. I settle on *Divergent*. Theo James is hot, and that kiss he puts on Shailene Woodley is incredible. Maybe daydreaming about Theo doing that to me will help dull the ache Gunner has left in my heart.

But Theo's voice reminds me of Gunner's, and before I know it, I'm heartsick again.

I still don't know why Gunner waited all this time to be with me. Our midnight rendezvous could all just be for a notch in his bedpost. Maybe all I am is a conquest, and once he returns to Ohio State, he'll shack back up with whatever girl he's moved on to since his last girlfriend, the Libra who was no good for him. Or maybe he'll go back to her. After all, he's a free man. He can do whatever he wants.

And here I thought he would make love to me tonight. Fat chance of that happening now.

My phone vibrates on my nightstand as I set down the TV remote.

When I pick it up, heat blasts through me. It's Gunner.

Where'd you go? I've been looking everywhere for you.

I ignore his question and ask one of my own.

Why are you looking for me?

Less than a minute later, he replies.

I found a room upstairs where we can sneak away to be alone for a little while.

Really? He's got some balls.

You mean the room I saw you coming out of with Simone?

I wait so long for him to reply that I begin to think he's not going to.

Where are you?

He's not even going to try to explain what I saw. I'm not sure if I respect him for not trying to lie about what happened by telling me it wasn't what I thought, or if I'm more hurt that he didn't at least apologize.

I'm at home.

Nothing. For ten minutes, I get no reply. Fifteen. Twenty. Simone must have gotten her hands back on him.

I abandon any hope that he's going to text me back and try to focus on the movie, but it's hopeless. I'm too hurt to focus on anything other than replaying the nights I've shared with him, and then how I saw him leaving that bedroom with Simone.

And . . . I'm crying again.

I thought I had finally found something special with Gunner. Not only have I never had sex, but I've never even had a boyfriend. All these years, everything has been about Gunner. My heart, my soul, my entire life has belonged to him even though he never knew it. And just when I thought he felt the same way, I'm slapped with the reality that I've been nothing but a pastime.

I have no idea how, but eventually I fall asleep.

When I awaken, it's still dark outside, my TV is still on, and I'm clutching my other pillow like it's Gunner's body.

Just as I begin to tighten my hold on the pillow and burrow more deeply into its plush softness, I freeze. Someone is sitting on my bed. I can tell by the way the mattress dips behind me.

My eyes flash open, and I hold my breath. That's when I feel the hand resting on my hip.

I don't need to roll over to see who's with me.

The silence stretches between us as if he's waiting for me to roll over.

When I don't, he says, "It took me longer than I thought it would to find a ride back here."

How long has he been sitting on my bed waiting for me to wake up?

"Why are you here?" I hadn't thought he would come to me tonight. I'm both excited and confused as to why he has.

His palm slides higher on my hip, and he gives it a gentle tug, trying to persuade me to face him. "Cami, look at me."

My eyes feel like I've sprayed them with hairspray. They're gritty and irritated. I don't want him to see I've been crying, so I tuck myself more securely against my pillow, resisting the temptation to look at him.

"Come on, Cami, look at me."

"You were with her, weren't you?" The backs of my eyes sting, but I fight back the tears.

"Who? Simone?" He sounds truly confused. "No. No, Cameron, I wasn't *with* her. I haven't been *with* her in a long time." Now he sounds frustrated.

"But I saw you," I say accusingly. "You were coming out of that bedroom with her."

I sound like a jealous girlfriend, but I don't care. I know we aren't a couple, and I know he can see, kiss, and screw whoever he wants, but I think he should have made that clear before he went off and did it. He owed me that much.

His hand is still on my hip, and my body betrays me by liking how it feels.

"Nothing happened," he says.

Why is he lying? Does he think he's protecting my feelings? I've got news for him, it's too late for that. My feelings have already been trampled.

"I know Simone's your ex-girlfriend, Gunner. If you want to get back together with her, that's fine. I get it. She's gorgeous, and I'm—"

He whips me to my back, abruptly stealing my words as he bends forward and kisses me. "Beautiful," he says, his gaze piercing mine. "You're absolutely, incredibly beautiful. The only reason I ever went out with Simone in the first place was because your brother would have kicked my ass if I had tried to go out with you."

His midnight-ocean-blue eyes swim in my vision. "What?" My voice sounds so small.

The corners of his mouth tip upward. "Do I finally have your attention?"

"Yes." I still sound like a mouse, skittish and frail.

"Good, because I'm only going to say this one more time." He drops a light, lingering kiss on my lips. "Nothing." He kisses me again. "Happened." Another kiss. "Tonight." One more kiss. "There is nothing going on between me and Simone. I broke up with her two years ago." His lips brush over mine yet again. "I never should have gone out with her in the first place, because my heart only wanted you." I'm starting to like these kisses. "I've always liked you." Kiss. "When you were younger, I thought you were cute." My body is warming. "I had such a huge crush on you." His body seems to be warming, too. "Didn't you ever wonder why I spent so much time here?"

This time, he doesn't kiss me. He holds himself up on his elbows, watching me, waiting for an answer.

What was his question? Oh, yeah. Why he spent so much time here when we were kids.

"I just assumed you were here for Nick."

"Well, yeah. We were friends. But I always wanted us to come over here instead of going to my house because *you* were here." He brushes back my hair.

What is he saying? That's he's liked me as long as I've liked him?

"So . . . Simone . . .?" I search his face.

"One of those two silly girls who followed me around all night spilled a glass of punch on the back of her blouse, and I went with her to help clean out the stain."

I suddenly feel about as silly as a clown at a funeral.

"I swear, Cami, that's all there was to it. I talked about you the whole time I was with her."

"You did?"

"Yes." He grins and lets out a breathy snort. "I

talked about you so much she probably started to wonder if I've done anything *but* think about you for the past year."

My heart starts beating faster. "What did you tell her?"

"How funny you are. How sweet. And smart. And talented. How I hope you go to Ohio State next year so we can be together." He halts, searching my face. "How I'm in love with you."

A second ago, my heart was racing. Now it feels like it's totally stopped. Either that or it's beating so fast it just *feels* like it's stopped. "You're in love with me?"

His dark eyes glisten from the light coming off the TV. "Cameron, I think I've loved you since I met you. It just took me awhile to figure it out."

Oh my God. I got everything all wrong tonight. He wasn't messing around with Simone. Gunner loves me. *Me!* I misjudged the situation, him, me, us . . . all of it.

Words can't express how I feel. Frenzied elation rockets through me, as does feverish anticipation.

I don't want this moment to slip by, not when I've waited so long for it.

Slapping my palm around the back of his neck, I bring his face to mine and fuse my lips to his in a gut-twisting kiss. One full of our tongues dancing together, blistering heat, and determination. When I break away, my gaze locks to his. "Make love to me."

He searches my face as if looking for doubt. When he finds none, his jaw clenches with resolve, and he pushes off the bed.

"I'll be right back." He darts to his room.

While he's gone, I take off my clothes. Tossing them to the floor, I demurely pull the sheet over my body and hold it to my chest. I may be ready to have sex with Gunner, but I can't dismiss my shyness around him quite so easily.

He's back within seconds and tosses a pair of square plastic packages on my nightstand. Condoms.

This is really happening. I'm going to lose my virginity tonight, and I'm giving it to the only man I ever want to be with. I don't care how many girls he's slept with. It's not important anymore. The only thing that's important is that he loves me, and I want to celebrate that revelation giving my body to his.

Standing beside the bed, he takes off his shirt and jeans, adding them to my clothes on the floor, but he leaves on his underwear. Even so, I can see his excitement jutting from between his legs, straining the fabric of his briefs.

"You're sure about this?" he asks as he climbs into bed with me, pushing back the sheet to kneel between my legs.

I'm bared to him, stripped not just of my clothes but of all pretense.

"Yes."

I'm nervous, eager, and scared all at once. I've

heard it hurts the first time, but I refuse to chicken out. I want this. Nothing is going to stop me from taking this moment all the way.

"I'll be gentle," he reassures me, stroking his fingers up and down my legs.

All I can do is nod and gulp air past the cotton in my mouth.

"Just relax." His soft, deep voice lulls me as his palms glide high on the inside of my thighs.

My skin sizzles, and it feels like the bottom just fell out of my stomach as the tips of his fingers come within inches of the heart of me. So close, but so far away as his hands retreat toward my knees.

"Aren't you going to take off your underwear?" I ask, reaching for the elastic band that reads "DIESEL" around his waist.

He takes my hand and presses it against the mattress. "Not yet. Not until you're ready."

"But I *am* ready." I try to reach for his shorts again, but he holds down my arms, bending forward so his face is directly above mine.

"Your mind is ready," he says, "but I want your body ready, Cameron. You're a virgin. This won't be any fun for either of us if your body isn't ready for me first. I don't want to hurt you."

Oh. I never thought about that. "How do I get my body ready then?"

He grins, and I swear he looks like the devil. A very sexy devil. He slowly lowers his face until his lips touch mine. "Getting you ready is *my* job."

Warmth blossoms inside my stomach and creeps outward, spreading through my arms and legs.

"How will you know when my body is ready?" I've taken sexual education and read enough books to know the answer to my question. I just want to hear *his* answer.

He chuckles and slides his mouth down the center of my stomach, sending shock waves through my muscles. I quiver as his mouth brushes against my sex before he rises onto his knees again.

"I'll know because you'll be good and wet. Right here." His fingers slide between my labia, and I suck in my breath. "Mmm, you're already wet."

I smile at the way his eyes twinkle in the darkness. "So does that mean I'm ready?"

"Not yet." His fingers traipse down my thighs, tickling my skin and making desire flame through my soul. "Now I need to make you beg for it."

I let out a frustrated groan. "Pleeeeaaasse."

He releases another dark chuckle as he shakes his head and glides his palms up my thighs again. "Not that kind of begging. Now . . . sssshhhh. Let me do this the way I always imagined I would."

The way he always imagined? Is it possible he's fantasized about this moment as long as I have?

I'm hot inside, slick between my legs, and tingling all over, poised at the tip of the needle. Aroused isn't even the word for how I feel. I don't know how much readier I can be, but this is Gunner's game. If he wants to do this his way, I'll let him. I trust him, and he seems to know what he's doing, while I have no idea.

He stops and leans over me, grabbing the TV remote from the nightstand. He studies it for a moment then aims it over his head. The TV clicks off, casting my bedroom into total darkness.

"How about some music?" He rolls off the bed and retrieves his jeans from the floor. He fishes his phone out of his pocket.

"Sure."

He brings up his playlist. A few seconds later, "Little Things" by One Direction begins playing.

I love this song. It's on my own playlist, and every time I hear it, I think of Gunner.

He folds his hand around mine as Zayn Malik sings about hands fitting together as if it's meant to be. Mirroring the lyrics, Gunner slides his fingers around mine.

I stare at our joined hands.

His fingers are strong and firm. They're long and thick next to mine, which are short and slender. He has man hands.

That's when it hits me. I mean, it *really* hits me. He's not a boy anymore. I'm not a girl. We were when we met, but between then and now, we've grown up. We're a man and a woman, and we're about to take a step in our relationship there will be no coming back from. Once we do this, everything will be different.

What we've done every night before tonight has been nothing compared to what we're about to do.

Letting go of my hand, he eases his way onto my body as One Direction continues singing about the little things, and I pull him to me.

"I want this with you," I whisper just as he's about to kiss me.

"I want this with you, too," he whispers back.

And then his mouth is on mine. Our lips twist together, fusing, tugging, devouring. His tongue sweeps over mine, and a moan breaks from his chest as I slide my hand down his bare back, dipping my fingers inside the waist of his undershorts.

He brushes his fingers over my face, my neck, my arms. Then he grips my hands and presses them against the mattress on either side of my shoulders as he releases my mouth and kisses his way to my breast.

When he lets go of my hands to caress my slight curves, I grip the back of his head, digging my fingers into all that soft, thick hair, holding his mouth to my breast. The breath gasps out of me as his teeth scrape my nipple.

I'm rising, spinning, tightening everywhere. Heat blasts through me, pulsing like a beacon between my legs as he rolls his hips.

Rocking against him, sparks fire inside my core, and I draw in my breath, hoping he touches me there. He doesn't disappoint. His fingers slide down, finding me. He groans, parting my slick folds before swirling the tip of his middle finger around my clit.

I don't know how much readier I need to be, because I feel like I'm about to blast off.

He raises up and shifts side to side, and then I feel his bare hardness on me as he lowers himself again. He's shoved down his undershorts, freeing his erection.

I open my eyes to find him staring down at me. He's watching me, drinking in my reaction.

Wanting him to know I'm more than ready to feel him, I wrap my arms around his shoulders and encircle his hips with my legs. I rock against him and drag my core up his shaft to the very tip, where I stop and hold myself as if daring him to take the next step.

His forehead is damp. Tiny beads of perspiration have formed on his naturally tan skin. His heavy breaths meet mine, and we're both poised right on the edge where love and desire meet.

The head of his cock glides lower, and I hold my breath. He's right there. If he pushes forward, he'll be inside me. He makes a noise deep inside throat, and I know he wants to keep going. That he feels the coiled energy between us the same as I do.

"Jesus," he murmurs, pulling away and thrusting his hand toward the top of the nightstand, retrieving one of the condoms.

He kicks off his undershorts then tears open the packet. I've never seen a condom before, and I stare as he hurriedly rolls it on.

Giving it a tug at the tip, he comes down on top of me again, his mouth crashing against mine as a moan rumbles out of his throat. I rock my hips against him, needing more. My body seems to have taken over my mind. Everything is centered around what's happening between my legs. The heat. The swollen need. The greedy desire to pull him inside me and feel what I've only read about in books.

"Now . . . please . . ." I'm more than ready. I know I am.

His hand shoots between us, and he lifts his hips. Then I feel the sheathed head of his cock stroke me up and down. I gasp as fiery explosions detonate throughout my body.

He's inside me. Just a little. Just the tip.

I clutch his back, pulling, moaning, squirming for more.

He eases forward, and I feel a pinch. I tense and inhale abruptly as I utter a quiet but alarmed squeak. He stops, giving me a moment.

"Are you okay?" Concern fills his eyes.

I nod. I feel so full, and he's not even all the way in. Licking my lips, I pant through the fading pain and meet his eyes. "I'm fine. Don't stop."

This is it. I'm letting go of the last piece of my innocence. Only one man can possess my virginity, and I've always wanted that man to be Gunner. My fantasy is finally coming true.

"Relax," he says, smoothing his fingers over my

face. "Keep breathing and relax."

I try to do what he says, but I'm too excited to relax. I just want him inside me. All the way inside. I want to feel his body meet mine.

Tiny whimpers ride the staccato exhales pushing out of me.

"Ssshhh . . ." He kisses me, sweeping his tongue past my lips, causing the most incredible feeling to surge through my inner muscles, which are stretched around him.

I'm flooded with warmth, and I moan into his mouth.

"That's it," he says, coaxing me, pushing deeper. "God, you're so tight."

There's discomfort but not pain. Just this unusual stretching that I'm not accustomed to. Nothing as big as what he's giving me has ever been inside me. As far as I'm concerned, Gunner has the biggest cock in the world.

The front of his hips meet my body, and he lets out a luscious sigh. "God, you feel good."

That's it? He's in? All the way?

That wasn't' so bad.

He barely moves, slowly rocking his hips, pressing fully against me.

"Are you still okay?" he asks, his voice breathy and urgent.

"Yes." Surprisingly, it's starting to feel good. Strange. Tight. But good. I smile and slide my arms farther around his back. "What about you?"

His breath hitches with amusement, and he gives me a broken, lopsided grin. "I'm *very* okay." He begins moving with more certainty.

Now that he knows he's not hurting me, he seems more confident, getting more into it. And now that I'm getting used to how it feels to be full of Gunner, I'm starting to loosen up.

I'm not sure I'll be able to have an orgasm, but it doesn't hurt as much as I thought it would. Maybe because he did such a good job preparing me.

He begins sliding in and out. His strokes are shallow at first, and then they elongate, growing more energetic, deeper, gruffer.

The noises he makes intensify. His moans turn into groans then into growls, and finally into a steady roll of grunts as his body slaps against mine.

"Gunner!" I hold on with everything I have. My body sings, awakened to a new type of pleasure. I'm not having an orgasm, but watching him lose control, knowing I'm the one doing that to him, fills me with awestruck wonder bordering on bliss.

Moments later, his body seizes, and he lets out a prolonged groan that sounds like a tight exhale. He's holding me, pumping his hips in shallow thrusts, grunting and uttering my name in my ear. "Cami . . . oh my God, Cami."

When his orgasm subsides, he pushes up to look into my eyes. His are glazed. He's panting, and then a wondrous grin pops over his mouth, lighting up his whole face.

"What?" I smile up at him, saying one last good-bye to my virginity as it locks itself inside his soul.

"Nothing. Just . . ."

I bite my lip, waiting.

"I never thought it would be that good."

We gaze into each other's eyes for a few seconds, and then he gently pulls out of me.

The emptiness feels foreign now that he's molded me to his shape and size, but I don't have long to miss his fullness as he slides down my body.

"What are you doing?"

He kisses his way down my stomach. "Taking care of you."

"What do y — ?" I cut off as he clamps his mouth on me, rapidly flicking his tongue over my clit.

Throwing my head back, I grip his head and cry out. My orgasm is already flying toward home base. I'm seconds from blowing apart. Having sex has helped me discover a whole new set of nerve endings.

"Gunner, Gunner . . . oh God!" He's given me a lot of orgasms in the last week, but this one is going to put them all to shame.

His tongue, his mouth, the heat and slick wetness. I can't breathe. I can't move. I can't make a single sound as every muscle in my body pulls in on itself.

And then . . .

I explode.

Losing all sense of where I am and what's happening to me, all I can do is give in to the pleasure ripping through me.

So this is what all the fuss is about? I've heard the other kids at school talk about it, and I've read about it in my dirty books, but now I get it. This right here . . . this moment. The euphoria lifting me to another plane is why girls dream about this moment all their lives and cry when their boyfriends break up with him. It's why God made orgasms, so that we mere mortals can get a glimpse of the joy that awaits us when we die, because what I'm feeling this very second is surely how it feels in heaven.

When I finally come back down to earth, I open my eyes to find Gunner over me, holding himself up, watching my face intently, a smile stretching from ear to ear.

"Did you like that?"

That is still happening. My legs and arms still quiver every few seconds as aftershocks ricochet through my body, and my heart beats at a frenzied tempo.

"Yes." The word comes out more as a breath than a part of speech.

His smile grows wider. and he gives me a long, tender kiss. No tongue this time. He joins his lips with mine and holds himself there while I revel in the pulsing energy lingering in my body.

It's official. I really *am* a woman now.

Chapter 8

"How many times have you done that?" I ask.

He's lying next to me, holding my hand, stroking my fingers with his. It's been at least five minutes since my breathing returned to normal, and we've simply been staring up at the ceiling in silence, throwing each other occasional glances filled with secret giddiness. It's as if neither of us can believe what just happened.

He lets out a refreshed sigh and smiles. "Actually, I've *never* done *that*."

I frown. "Are you saying . . .? You weren't a virgin, too, were you?"

He lets go of my hand and rubs his palm down his face before rolling onto his side to face me. "No. I'm not a virgin. What I meant was that what I've done with other girls doesn't even come close to what we just did."

I hold his gaze for a long time, both thrilled and nervous.

"How many girls have there been?" I finally ask.

Shadows pass through his eyes. "A few. I won't

lie, there have been other girls, Cameron. Not many, but enough for me to know what I'm doing."

I assumed there had been, so this doesn't surprise me. What *does* surprise me is how much I don't like hearing him talk about it. But just because I don't like it doesn't mean I don't need to hear it. I do. Especially when he said that what he did with the girls who came before doesn't compare to what he and I just did. And, honestly, after how he just made me feel, I can't be jealous of how he gained his experience.

"How is what we did different from the other girls?"

He takes hold of my hand again, sliding his fingers between mine. "It just was." He offers me a compassionate smile. "The other girls I've been with never made me feel special. I felt more like a conquest." He lies back down but keeps his head turned toward me. "Sex with someone who just wants sex is like trying to take a drink from an empty glass. Sex with you felt like I was drinking from a fountain." He chuckles. "I just had no idea how thirsty I was."

I smile and prop myself on my elbow. "What makes sex with me so special?"

"I don't know. Maybe because of how I feel about you. Because when you want something as long as I've wanted you, it's like winning the lottery when you finally get it."

"Why didn't you ever say anything?" I ask, running my other hand up his ripped stomach.

College has done his physique good. He was always hot, but now he's even hotter.

"Nick," he says.

"Nick?"

"I didn't want my best friend kicking my ass for putting the moves on his little sister."

"He's still your best friend," I remind him.

"I know, but I'm done holding myself back for fear of what your brother will do to me. I've tried to like other girls. I've tried to honor you as my best friend's little sister by staying away. But I'm done with that shit. I refuse to live in fear of Nick kicking my ass, anymore." He rolls me to my back and settles partially on top of me, one of his legs slung over mine. The sole of his foot caresses my calf. "You don't want that, do you?"

"What? Nick kicking your ass? Or you staying away because you're afraid he will?"

"Look at you, getting all smart-mouthed now that I've fucked you."

I gasp. "Gunner!"

He laughs, and I love the sound. I also love the way his chest vibrates against mine. "I'm only kidding." He tilts his head. "I mean, technically, we did fuck, but I don't like how that word feels for what just happened between us."

Honestly, I don't either. What happened between Gunner and me was too special to call fucking.

I smile and trail my palms up his arms to his

shoulders. "To answer your question, no, I don't want you to stay away because of my brother."

I'm a little upset to learn that Nick was his reason for not revealing his feelings sooner. To think we could have been doing this years ago. It's almost criminal that we robbed ourselves of all that time.

He slides off me and rolls to his back again, raking his hair off his forehead. "I can't believe you never knew I liked you."

"*I* can't believe you never knew *I* liked *you*."

He throws me an incredulous glance. "You did?"

"Duh."

"Seriously?"

"Yeah. From the moment I met you." Did he really not know? "I thought it was obvious."

The expression on his face as he turns his gaze back to the ceiling is one of bewilderment. No doubt he's doing the math inside his head to figure out how long we could have been playing doctor with one another.

"I never realized," he says. "Then again"—he tosses me a cheesy smile—"I'm a big dumb guy. I'm clueless when it comes to girls liking me."

"Well, I guess I'm just as clueless, because I thought you never even noticed me. I thought I was just Nick's baby sister to you."

He rolls to his side and props himself on his elbow, brushing my hair off my face. "No. You were never just Nick's baby sister." He gazes at me for the longest time, and then a goofy smile breaks over his face. "There was this one time during the summer before my sophomore year when I was out riding bikes with Nick. It was really hot, and we ended up coming back to your house to get into the air conditioning. We pedaled our ten-speeds into the driveway, and there you were, practicing free throws. You had gotten your hair cut short earlier in the day. Do you remember that?"

I do and wince. "Ugh, yes. I hated that haircut." I remember being embarrassed when he saw me.

"I know you did, but I thought it was cute. It made you look older." His palm slides down my long blond hair. "Don't get me wrong, I love your hair longer, especially now, but back then, seeing it shorter made me see you in a whole new way."

I'm suddenly grateful for the haircut I hated but caught his eye.

"I already had a crush on you," he continues, "but that day, I think my crush turned into something more. Infatuation maybe. I don't know what to call it. I just know it was stronger than a crush.

"Anyway, Nick and I rode our bikes up the driveway, and you shot a free throw and missed then rushed up and grabbed the rebound and took it in for a layup. I thought that was so sexy.

"Watching you play basketball always turned me on. Don't ask me why. I think I just liked seeing you get all sweaty and messy. It was different from how the other girls were. They always had to have every hair in place and their makeup perfect. It's like they thought perspiration was this terrible, horrible thing. And there you were, covered in sweat, your hair falling out of your ponytail and sticking to your face and the back of your neck. God, seeing you like that was such a turn-on." He sighs and traces my jaw with his fingertip. "Tonight at the party reminded me of that day."

"It did?"

"Oh yeah." He nods dramatically.

"How?"

"Seeing you dancing. You're a great dancer, by the way. I've never seen you dance like that."

I flash him a coy glance. "It's the new me."

"I like it. But yeah, you were all sweaty, and all I wanted to do was join you on the dance floor and lick your skin."

"Sounds kinky." Grown-up Gunner is a bit of a freak. He likes me sweaty. I'll have to remember that.

That sly grin breaks over his face again. "I might be a little kinky." He winks at me. "Not much, though. Is that going to be a problem?"

Is he kidding? We just had sex, and I loved every second of it. Then again, maybe he didn't show me his particular brand of kinky. "I guess that depends."

"On what?"

"What you consider kinky."

His expression grows mischievous. "Whips,

candle wax, bondage. That sort of thing."

My eyes go wide and my mouth falls open. "I . . . I'm not sure —"

He laughs. "I'm only kidding." He scoots closer, making the space around us more intimate. "I might spank you when I take you from behind, though."

"From behind?"

"You know, doggie style."

I know "from behind" and "doggie style" are the same thing. I'm just surprised he's already thinking about doing that with me. It's as if he's already fantasized about it.

His palm trails down to my wrist, and he lifts my forearm. "Maybe I'll put a blindfold on you or tie your wrists with a scarf or something. I've never done that before."

"You haven't?"

He shakes his head as his fingers caress my wrist. He meets my gaze and grins. "I'd like to try it."

I've read about men who blindfold women and tie them up during sex, and I'll admit such ideas have found their way into my own fantasies. "What if I don't like it?"

"Then we won't do it." He takes hold of my opposite arm and rolls to his back, pulling me with him so I'm snuggled against his side.

I settle my head on his chest. My arm rests across his stomach, and his fingers are lazily caressing it.

I still can't believe we just had sex. I don't really

feel different. I thought losing my virginity would be more grandiose and that I would feel older or more womanly or something. But I still feel the same. Just happier, because the person I had sex with is the one I always wanted.

Out of all the girls he could have chosen, he picked me. It blows my mind.

"Why me?" I ask quietly.

"What do you mean?"

I push myself onto my elbow. "You could have anyone, Gunner. Why me?"

He frowns like my question upsets him. "Why *not* you?"

I sit up and pull the blankets over my lap. "Well, because . . ." I think about it for a moment. "Because I'm not one of *those* girls. You know, the ones with the perfect hair and the perfect makeup."

He lets out an incredulous laugh. "I thought we already settled this. I don't want perfect. Perfect is boring."

"Well, I'm a dork. I'm a total geek. I get straight A's." That's got to be as boring as perfection.

He scoots closer and smiles as if appeasing me. "Smart girls are sexy. Next." He gives me a cool expression that says he's ready to dispel every reason I could possibly throw at him for why I can't believe he would choose me over someone else.

I point to my trumpet case sitting on the floor by my desk. "I play in the band." I say it like I'm challenging him.

He relaxes and rests his head on his hand. "Haven't you heard that trumpet players make the best kissers?"

I huff and cock my head. "You just made that up."

"No I didn't." He sits up and faces me. "It's true. Google it." He grabs his phone from my nightstand, cutting off the music. He opens a Google search on his phone then activates the microphone to ask, "Do trumpet players make the best kissers?" His phone chimes, and he begins reading from the first result that pops up in the search results.

I cut him off. "That doesn't prove anything."

"Of course it does. It proves I'm right."

I roll my eyes. "No it doesn't."

He tosses his phone to the side and pushes me onto the bed, holding me down as he kisses me breathless. When he breaks away, he grins. "Then ask *me*."

"Ask you what?"

"If trumpet players make the best kissers."

"Why?"

"Just do it."

I huff, a little irritated that he stopped kissing me when I was starting to get worked up again. "Fine. Are trumpet players the best kissers?"

"Yes. Absolutely." He briefly finds my mouth again then nudges my nose with his as he breaks away. "Because you're the best kisser I've ever known." He kisses me again, letting his lips play over mine. Then he pulls away. "Speaking of trumpets, I haven't told you about my tattoo, yet, have I?"

I perk up. Honestly, I'd forgotten about it. I've seen it every night, but it's always too dark to make out what it is. All I know is that it takes up his shoulder and part of his left pectoral.

"No."

He sits up and grabs his phone again, turning on the flashlight.

I shield my eyes at the sudden brightness. When I open them again and adjust to the light, I study the swirls of ink.

His tattoo is a musical staff wrapped around itself in a distorted figure eight. There's a treble clef, musical notes, rest signs, flats and sharps, all created with an artistic flourish.

"Music?"

"Music set in an infinity loop." He looks down at his shoulder, tracing the tip of his finger around the figure eight. "The musical notes signify all the ups and downs we've had and will continue to have as we move forward, because I'm sure we'll go through our share of rough patches as we figure out this new direction we've taken in our relationship." He meets my gaze again. "But the infinity loop symbolizes that my feelings for you will never change."

I'm flattered and touched, but we've only just started down this new path. What if he does change his mind in a month or two? A year?

"How do you know your feelings will never change?"

"Cameron, I've felt this way about you for years. Do you really think that's going to change now?"

I press my palm against his ink. "I don't know, but getting a tattoo is awfully permanent."

"Exactly."

"What do you mean?"

He turns off the light and eases down on top of me again, stroking my face. "That's how strong my feelings are for you. To me, they *are* permanent." He stares into my eyes for the longest time, running the backs of his fingers over my cheek. "Cameron, sometimes you just know."

He's so warm and solid against me. So real. I'm definitely not dreaming. "Know what?"

"When you've found the person you're meant to be with."

Is he talking about now or forever? Did Gunner just tell me he thinks we're meant to be together for the rest of our lives?

I had no idea he felt this way about me.

I brush my hand over his shoulder. "Maybe *I* should get a tattoo."

One side of his mouth lifts. "Maybe you should."

"Where?"

He lifts on his arms and drinks me in with his eyes, studying my body. "That all depends."

"On what?"

"The tattoo you want to get."

"I don't know." I've never thought about it. "What do you think? A dragon? A butterfly?"

He seems to consider this for a moment then smirks and shakes his head. "A trumpet."

His levity shatters the serious mood, and I laugh. "A trumpet?"

He laughs with me. "Sure, why not? I've got the notes. You can have the trumpet. And together, we can make beautiful music." He lowers himself on top of me again and seals his lips over mine for a simmering kiss to prove his point about exactly what type of beautiful music he wants to make with me.

When he breaks away, I wind my hands around the back of his neck. "*You* didn't play trumpet."

A quizzical expression crosses his face. "So?"

"I just wanted to point that out since you made such a big deal about telling me that trumpet players make good kissers."

He grins, because he can tell there's more to it than that. "Oh? And why is that?"

I dig my fingers into his hair. "Because you're a good kisser, too."

"And your point is?"

"I don't think playing the trumpet has anything to do with it."

He smirks. "Is that your way of telling me to kiss you again?"

I nod. "Yes, please."

"That could be dangerous."

"Why?"

"Because if I start kissing you, I'm going to want to make love to you again."

"Then definitely kiss me."

He laughs. It's an aroused, I'm-about-to-do-bad-things laugh. "You're already going to be sore tomorrow, Cami."

"Then you might as well make it worthwhile."

He searches my eyes as the grin melts out of his expression, leaving only sincerity and desire. His erection presses against my leg.

"Don't say I didn't warn you." He grabs the other condom off the nightstand.

Chapter 9

Gunner was right. I am sore.

During my morning shower, I hiss at the burn of soap as it finds my bruised flesh. My thighs are sore, too. Like I used muscles I've never used before.

Gunner might have gotten a little rough the second time we had sex last night. I'm not complaining. This is just what it feels like to officially be a woman. Not just in age but in sexuality, too.

I loved everything we did last night. He had to use his mouth on me again to get me off the second time, and it took longer, but by the time I fell asleep, I had a smile the size of California on my face.

I'm still smiling, despite the discomfort between my legs.

After drying my hair and getting dressed, I make my way downstairs, aware of the satisfying ache in my thighs and deep inside my core.

Gunner is already sitting at the breakfast bar eating a bowl of cereal. Our eyes meet, and my face instantly heats. He bites back a smile and turns his gaze back to his breakfast.

My mom is making coffee and looks exhausted.

"Did you just get home?" I ask her as I fish milk and eggs from the fridge.

"About twenty minutes ago," she says, staring at the coffee maker like it needs to give her coffee before she loses her patience and smashes the thing into nothing more than a paper weight.

I grab a mixing bowl and a loaf of sourdough bread from the pantry, along with cinnamon. "You look awful."

She sneers at me. "Thanks." She turns back to the coffee maker. "Remind me again why I never drink."

I start slicing the bread on a cutting board. "Because you have no tolerance and hate the taste."

She snaps her fingers. "Oh yeah, that's right."

"The burning question of the hour, Mom, is if you don't like alcohol, why did you get drunk?"

"Because they had these fancy drinks that tasted like fruit punch instead of alcohol, and by the time I realized what they were, I'd had six of them."

Gunner and I exchange glances and start laughing. "You what?"

My mom holds up her hand. "Can you please not laugh right now? Or breathe? Or make any noise at all?"

The coffee maker finally sputters out the last of the coffee. I don't know why she doesn't just break down and buy a Keurig. She'd get her coffee a lot faster, but she says those K-cup thingies fill up landfills. My mom tries to be very conscious about the environment. We have recycling bins for everything from plastic to aluminum to food scraps she uses for composting.

"What are you doing?" she asks after taking a gingerly sip of her coffee. She just realized I'm making french toast.

"I'm making breakfast," I say proudly. "Hungry?"

She grimaces and her face turns a little green. "Maybe later."

She parks herself on the barstool at the end of the breakfast bar and watches me whisk eggs and milk together then sprinkle in cinnamon. I soak thick pieces of sourdough in the mixture while the griddle pan heats.

Gunner finishes his cereal and pushes the empty bowl aside. He doesn't appear any more eager than my mom to leave.

A few minutes later, as I drop the first slices of bread on the griddle, sending up a sizzle from the hot metal, my mom says, "What's gotten into you this morning?"

"What do you mean?" I ask.

"You never make breakfast."

I glance at Gunner and feel my blush response fire up again. Having sex with him made me feel like a true grown-up for the first time in my life. And grown-up women cook breakfast, especially for the men they love.

I shrug, fishing a spatula out of the drawer beside the stove, keeping my back to my mom so she doesn't see the evidence of what he and I did last night on my face.

"I just wanted to make us breakfast this morning, Mom. That's all." I glance at Gunner. "Do you want some."

His gaze dances delightfully as he nods and pushes aside the cereal box. "I'd love some. Thanks."

I nibble my bottom lip as I turn back to the stove and flip the slices of French toast. Gunner is definitely going to get some. He got some last night, and if I have my way, he'll get some again tonight.

* * *

I don't get my way. Gunner comes to me, but instead of having sex, we hold hands, make out like crazy, and more or less watch a movie. Actually, less. We spend more time kissing and groping than actually paying attention to what's happening on TV. But he says he doesn't want to have sex because he doesn't want to hurt me. I *am* sore, so I see his point. But I'm still disappointed.

However, the next night, we do have sex again. As well as the following night. I think both of us look forward to bedtime more than we ever have in our lives.

This is how the days pass. During the day, we

maintain our distance, but at night, he comes to me and we have sex. He still has to finish me with his mouth, though. As excited as he gets me during sex, I haven't been able to come with him inside me. I don't really mind, because it all feels incredible, but it is frustrating. Why can he get me so worked up I'm practically shivering out of my skin, but I just can't quite reach orgasm?

On Christmas Eve, he comes to me later than usual. Joining me on the bed, he pulls a small, gift-wrapped box from the pocket of his hoodie.

"Merry Christmas," he says.

A gift? He bought me a Christmas gift?

"What's this?" I take the box from him. It's wrapped in shiny red paper decorated with tiny silver Christmas bulbs. A silver ribbon is tied in slightly flattened curlicues on top.

"Open it."

We keep our voices down in case my parents are still awake. No parties took them away from home tonight.

Nibbling the inside of my lip, I sit forward, crossing my legs, and eagerly snap the ribbon and tear the paper along the bottom seam.

"But I didn't get you anything." I crumple the paper and set it beside me.

"Yes you did."

I lift my gaze to his. "No, I—"

His crooked grin and the suggestive twinkle in his

eyes halts my words.

It dawns on me what he's saying. My gift to him was my virginity. "Oh." My face heats as I drop my gaze. "I see."

He tucks my hair behind my ear. "Best gift anyone has ever given me, by the way."

Warmth pours into my cheeks. "I'm glad you liked it. It's a one of a kind."

He slowly bends forward and presses a tender kiss to my cheek. "I'm honored you gave it to me," he says softly.

My fingers play with the edge of the small white box in my hand. I don't care what's inside. It could be a plastic decoder ring from a gumball machine for all I care. The important thing is that it came from him.

"Go ahead." He bobs his chin at the box. "Open it."

As butterflies take flight in my stomach, I lift the lid. Inside the box, resting on a bed of cotton, is a black leather Pandora charm bracelet.

I gasp.

"Gunner! This is too much." These bracelets and their charms aren't cheap. I know his family has money. So does mine. But he's a college student. He doesn't need to spend hundreds of dollars on a bracelet for me.

"Do you like it?" He sounds genuinely proud as I slowly lift it from the box.

"I love it, but—"

"Then it's not too much." He takes it from me. "Hold out your wrist."

Tucking my hair behind my ear with one hand, I extend the other in front of me.

I heard once that a man doesn't buy a woman jewelry unless he really loves her. I guess this settles any lingering doubts I might have had about how Gunner feels about me.

He secures the bracelet then starts explaining the charms. "There's a basketball"—he points out the silver basketball charm—"because of that time I saw you playing basketball and the effect it had on me." He slides a cupcake charm along the leather bangle. It's decorated with pale-pink enamel. "And this one is because I know how much you love cupcakes. It reminded me of that birthday party when you told your mom you didn't want a cake but a cupcake tower instead."

I giggle that he remembered that. It was my fourteenth birthday.

He points to a round charm with starfish and pale-blue stones on it. "This one reminded me of all the seashells you brought back from your vacation to the beach the summer before your freshman year. I missed you so much for the week you were gone," he says quietly. "And these"—he indicates a pair of silver charms that are side by side—"are for you and me. This one is for Scorpio, and this one is for Capricorn."

"Scorpio and Capricorn?" I never thought he was

into astrology.

He grins. "You and me, baby. Don't think I never noticed all those astrology books you read when we were kids. You were always reading your horoscope."

I laugh. "I never thought you noticed."

"Cami, I noticed *everything* about you."

He goes back to pointing out the last four charms.

"There's one here for music"—he gestures toward his tattoo as he glances at my trumpet, indicating that's why he got that charm—"and the one shaped like a Christmas gift to remind you of the Christmas break we just spent together. Then there's a flower, so you'll have flowers from me every day. And last is a heart." He takes my hand and squeezes it. "That charm is to remind you every time you look at it that my heart belongs to you."

I never took Gunner to be such a romantic. He's always been so quiet and mysterious. In a lot of ways, he still is, but bit by bit, his layers are peeling back, and he's revealing himself to me.

Every minute I spend with him makes clearer just how long he's liked me. His Christmas gift is proof of that. Each charm was selected for a specific memory, some representing incidents I'd almost forgotten but remained clear enough in his own mind to inspire his gift.

I'm touched, moved, and speechless.

I stare at the bracelet, examining each charm, hearing his voice in my head as he tells me what each one means. When I get back to the heart, I lift my gaze to his.

"Thank you. I love it."

He kisses me. "I'm glad." His lips meet mine again, this time for longer. "And there's plenty of room left for more charms. As we make more memories, I'll add to your collection."

I lean into him, my heart full of joy. He wants to make more memories with me. He's not thinking this is just a passing fling. Gunner sees us together beyond Christmas break. He hasn't said anything to make me think he only wanted our fling to last for the few short weeks he was home, but this bracelet says more than words ever could that he wants to be with me. As in, *be* with me. With no end date in mind.

"You know I can't wear this around my parents," I say, lifting my wrist to indicate the bracelet. "They'll ask questions, and I'll have to tell them about you."

They still don't know what's going on between Gunner and me. No one does. I told Julie a little more when I talked to her a couple of days ago, but even she doesn't know how far we've gone.

Gunner lies back with me on my bed and wraps his arms around me from behind, spooning me.

"I need to man up and tell Nick first."

"Do you really think he'll be mad?"

"I have no idea. But this other guy I know got the shit kicked out of him by the brother of the girl he was dating. And another guy warned his friends not to even try to get with his sister or he'd kick their asses. So I'm not feeling very good about how he'll react."

Who knew big brothers could be so protective of their little sisters? I've never gotten much of that vibe from Nick, but maybe Gunner has, which is why he's so wary about telling him about us.

The movie we're watching ends a few minutes later, and he sneaks back into his room, leaving me to gaze at the bracelet while hoping we'll be able to work this out before he returns to Ohio State.

I don't want to keep him a secret anymore.

* * *

The day after Christmas, I lie and tell my parents I'm spending the day at Julie's house, but the truth is I'm going to a movie with Gunner. The theater is packed. We sit in the back row, holding hands and stealing occasional kisses.

It feels like we're doing something bad by going out together. In a way, we are, because we're sneaking around, and I had to lie. I don't like lying to my parents.

After the movie, we tempt fate and stop for something to eat before going to his house, where we spend an hour in his childhood bedroom before returning to my house.

This is how the days pass, with us sneaking around, and before I know it, it's New Year's Eve. My midnight rendezvous with Gunner are almost over. He leaves in two days.

My parents are going to another party tonight. What can I say? They're popular people. But all those parties have been great, because they allowed me more time with Gunner.

Missy's family got back from her grandparents' house the day after Christmas, so Nick has been spending as much time with her as possible, and tonight is no exception. He's taking her to a party and probably won't be home until morning.

He invited Gunner to go with him, but Gunner begged off, saying he had other plans. What he didn't reveal was that those plans were with me.

To keep up appearances, Gunner left the house thirty minutes ago, pretending to be heading off to a party.

"Are you going to be all right here by yourself?" my mom asks as Dad helps her into her coat.

"Absolutely." I'm curled up on the couch with a blanket over my legs, watching a movie. Okay, so I'm only *pretending* to be watching a movie, since I've got a one-track mind that's totally focused on Gunner.

"You sure you don't want to ask Julie over?"

"I'm fine, Mom." I'll be even better once she, Dad, and Nick leave. "I'm not a party animal like you and Dad."

She sighs wistfully as she starts toward the door leading to the garage. "Your dad isn't a party animal, either. I think he's ready to be done with the holidays." She stops and smiles back at me. "But you might be onto something there. I'm about partied out, too." She blows me a kiss. "Order a pizza or something if you get hungry."

"Maybe." I wave. "Have fun."

"You, too, honey."

Dad kisses my cheek. "Happy New Year, Cam."

"You, too."

He follows Mom to the garage, and a couple of minutes later, Dad's Mercedes backs out of the driveway.

A few minutes later, Nick darts out the door.

I'm finally alone. The house is all mine for the rest of the night. Mine and Gunner's.

I pull out my phone and send Gunner a text.

Everyone's gone.

I hurry upstairs, change into my favorite pair of jeans, a light-blue blouse, and then nervously check my hair in the bathroom mirror. Once I'm satisfied with how I look, I spritz my wrists with perfume then put on my bracelet.

By the time I make my way back downstairs, Gunner's car is pulling into the driveway. He parks behind the house.

I open the back door, and he scoops me into a hug, kissing me. It's the first kiss we've shared in my house that wasn't in my bedroom, and it feels like we're breaking the rules. Like we're doing something taboo.

Which ramps up the arousal stirring low in my belly.

"Hey," he says, breaking away, his eyes twinkling.

"Hey." I draw my bottom lip between my teeth and shyly lower my gaze.

"It's too late for that," he says.

"For what?"

He grins. "For you to get shy on me."

I giggle and tuck my face against his chest, making him laugh.

"Come on," he says, "*Dick Clark's New Year's Rockin' Eve* is waiting."

There's leftover seven-layer dip in the fridge, so we grab that, a bag of corn chips, and build a pair of sandwiches using corned beef cold cuts. Then we head downstairs to the theater room, where we snuggle in the oversized leather chairs. As we eat, we talk about anything and everything while watching the countdown to midnight. I share my New Year's resolutions, and he shares his. We talk about school, sports, and music. The future. The past. No subject is off limits.

Kissing is a given. There's a lot of kissing. And touching. And maybe some groping.

Both of us know how the evening will end. With only a couple nights left before he leaves, we're not wasting any opportunity to explore the passion we've found with each other.

At five till midnight, we're making out like mad. We vowed to wait until midnight before having sex, but it's starting to look like we're not going to make it. My blouse is already a pool of discarded fabric in the chair next to us, leaving me in only my bra, panties, and unfastened jeans.

Gunner withdraws his lips from mine, but keeps our foreheads nestled together. "It's going to happen tonight."

I lower my gaze. "I hope so."

I still haven't come during sex. I've been close several times, but I can't quite get there.

"No," he says firmly but gently, lifting my chin and kissing me. "It will. I promise."

I want to believe him, but I'm not as confident as he is. For some reason, when we're having sex, I get right to the edge of orgasm and stop. Don't get me wrong, it feels incredible. I just want to feel what it's like to come with him inside me. The orgasms he gives me afterward are intense and wondrous, so I can only imagine how they would feel during the act rather than as an afterthought.

As the countdown to midnight reaches one minute, we start peeling off the rest of our clothes. His shirt. My jeans. His jeans. My bra. His undershorts. My panties.

How we're going to do this? The oversized theater chairs recline, but they don't recline to a flat position, which will make it awkward for him to be on top of me.

"Come here," he says before I have long to think about it.

He grabs me by the waist and pulls me onto his lap as he sits back down.

Oh. This is nice. I'm straddling him.

I rest my hands on his shoulders. "Do you want me on top?"

He's rolling on a condom he'd stashed in the pocket of his jeans.

"Yes." He grips my hip with one hand while stroking up his shaft with the other, tugging the condom the way he always does to ensure it's snug and that there's a little extra left at the tip.

The countdown hits ten seconds.

He pulls my hips forward and rubs the head of his erection front to back, slicking me while sending fragments of pleasure through my body.

My legs quiver with anticipation, and my fingers curl on his shoulders.

At five seconds, he directs the head of his cock to my entrance.

We wanted to start the new year together. As in, *together*. Joined as one.

"Ready?" he whispers.

I swallow a moan and nod, eager to be with him again. "Yes."

From the TV, I hear the crowd gathered in New

York cheer. They shout the final seconds of the year, counting them down, ready to greet the new.

As fireworks shoot off on the TV, I know it's here. I know the new year has begun.

Gunner pulls my mouth to his, and as we kiss, he thrusts upward as he drags me down onto him.

I gasp against his lips. This feels . . . different. He hits me at a new angle in this position. A more exciting angle. One that puts pressure on my inner muscles in just the right way. Maybe I *will* be able to come with him inside me tonight.

He's breathing hard, his lips barely touching mine as our gazes lock together.

"Fuck me," he mutters. "You're in control."

He says that like he likes me being in control. Like he wants me to do with him what I want. I can see the appeal. The tables have turned, and now he's the one who gets to lie back and experience the physical pleasure being given to him.

I roll my hips, uncertainly at first. He briefly closes his eyes and drops his head back, moaning.

His hands grip my hips and help churn me on him.

Using his guidance, feeling emboldened by his response, I rock against him more forcefully.

Oh my God, yes. He's hitting me just right. Exactly where I need him to hit me.

We find a rhythm, and within minutes I've gone from being unsure about this new position to riding him like I'm a rodeo cowgirl and he's the stallion I tamed from the open range.

And I feel it. I feel my orgasm rising, pushing forward, fighting to break free.

"Oh . . . oh my god . . ." It's right there. So close. Hovering.

He's staring up at me, watching me with taut eyes, grinding his teeth. "Are you going to come?" he bites out. He sounds like he's almost to the point of no return.

"I think so . . . I don't know . . . I'm so close." It feels like I'll explode any second. Like I'm just one thrust away from climaxing. But then I don't, and I'm one more thrust away. And then that one doesn't shake my orgasm free, either. What more can I do?

Gunner leans forward and clamps his mouth over my nipple, sucking hard.

Oh, Jesus!

That's it. That's all I need.

Crying out, the tide rises abruptly, the pleasure within me spiking. A split second later, I detonate.

All I am is one keening, tremulous wail as my body splinters, contracting and releasing against Gunner's cock.

Or maybe that's him, because he's coming, too. We're coming together. Ringing in the new year with a tremendous simultaneous orgasm, the likes of which I doubt the world has ever seen.

When it's over, I'm lying against Gunner like a dirty rag—boneless, motionless, and breathless.

His arms are around my back, holding me, keeping me close as he kisses my shoulder, my cheek, the corner of my mouth.

"I told you," he says.

I can't even muster the energy and mental acuity to reply. All I do is grunt.

I've never felt anything like that. Just . . . yeah, no words can do justice to what just happened to me.

I need a minute. Maybe five. Okay, ten.

And then I want to do it again.

Chapter 10

Two hours later, I'm on my stomach, my forehead resting on my hands on the floor in front of me, the weight of Gunner's body slung over my back.

Yes, I just came again. During sex. While Gunner took me from behind.

And I think I just found my new favorite position.

"I liked that," I say, still feeling the remnants of my orgasm ebbing and flowing through me.

"I could tell." He kisses the back of my shoulder.

We've had sex three times since midnight. And all three times I came.

I know why we're so desperate to have sex as much as possible. Neither of us wants to face his departure. But whether we face it or not, it's coming. All we can do is build as many memories as we can to get us through until we see each other again.

He sighs and pulls out of me, sliding off the condom and wadding it inside a tissue while I put on my panties and hunt down my blouse.

I freeze as I hear a noise come from upstairs.

Gunner stops moving, and his surprised eyes lock

with mine.

"If that's Nick, we're fucked," he whispers hotly.

We scatter, haphazardly pulling on our clothes and gathering the spent condom wrappers from the floor.

"Cameron!" My mom's voice comes from the top of the stairs, and panic sets in.

"Oh my God," I whisper. "It's my parents!"

If he thought we were fucked if Nick found us having sex, we're going to be crucified if my parents do.

We double our efforts to get dressed and clean up.

"Cameron, are you down there?"

"Mom? Is that you?" I run my fingers through my hair as I hear her high-heeled shoes thud dully on the carpeted stairs. God, my hair is all tangled. How am I going to pass off how I look?

Gunner stuffs the wadded-up condoms and wrappers in his pocket and points to the couch, indicating for me to lie down. He tosses me the pillow we used to prop under my stomach on the floor.

I catch it and collapse on the couch, tucking the pillow under my head while Gunner sprawls in the chair farthest from me, the bag of chips beside him and the TV remote in his hand.

A few seconds later, my mom appears in the doorway of the theater room.

"Mom? What are you doing home?" I lift onto my elbow and rub my eyes, pretending that I'd been asleep.

"Oh, hi, Gunner." My mom steps into the room. "I thought you went out tonight."

"I did." He grabs a corn chip and stuffs it in his mouth. "Got back about an hour ago and came down here to watch a movie. Cami was crashed on the couch." He winks at me. "The party animal."

My mom laughs and grabs a corn chip for herself. "Yes, that's our Cameron. Out by midnight every year."

Not *this* year.

I brush my hair off my face and rub my eyes again, really playing up the act. "I thought you and Dad were going to be out all night. Why are you home?"

Mom sighs. "Looks like your dad is partied out, too. He wanted to come home." She heads for the exit. "Honestly, I think he'll be happy if he doesn't see another party until *next* Christmas." She pauses at the door. "I just wanted to let you know we were home. We're heading up to bed."

"Okay. Good night."

"Good night, Gunner," my mom says as she walks out.

"Good night, Mrs. C." He waves over his shoulder even though she's already gone.

He meets my gaze but doesn't say anything. Neither of us do until we hear my mom reach the top of the stairs and everything goes silent.

"That was close," he says, letting out a relieved

exhale.

"Too close." I don't want my parents to know I'm having sex, but I don't want to keep my relationship with Gunner a secret from my family anymore, either. "We have to tell them," I say quietly.

"What? Now?"

"No, but tomorrow, okay. Let's tell them tomorrow."

His expression grows troubled.

"Gunner, things are just going to get more complicated until we tell them, no matter what happens with my brother."

"I know. You're right." But he doesn't look any more convinced than he did a few seconds ago.

Did he even plan to tell Nick? My parents? Anyone?

"Then what's holding you back?"

"Nothing."

I don't believe him.

He looks into the half-empty bag of corn chips. "I just don't want any complications."

"Neither do I. That's why it's time to tell them what's going on between us." Cold dread settles into my stomach. "Unless you're too afraid. Or maybe you're ashamed of me."

His eyes shoot to mine, and his thick eyebrows carve hard into his face. "I'm not ashamed of you."

"Then you're afraid."

"I'm not afraid."

"Aren't you? You're worried my brother will kick your ass. Is his opinion more important than mine? Is being scared of Nick and what he might do to you bigger motivation than how we feel about each other?"

He doesn't answer. He just sits there staring at me. And that says all I need to know.

What started out as the perfect beginning for the new year has been ruined by my parents' untimely return and Gunner's reaction. Have I made a mistake pouring my heart and soul into loving him? I want someone who will fight for me. A man who will protect me. And I don't just mean a man who will protect my body, but one who will protect my heart, my emotions, and every part of me.

Gunner has told me repeatedly that he's afraid Nick will kick his ass once he finds out what's going on between us. Is that more important than owning up to his feelings? Is his friendship with my brother more important than the love he claims to feel for me?

What others think shouldn't matter. I could understand if he wanted to hold onto our secret because he wants to keep the magic of *us* sacred. To hold onto the enchantment we've found by opening up to each other.

But that's not what he said. He's worried about Nick's reaction. He said he's scared Nick will kick his ass. And if he's scared of Nick's reaction, he's probably scared of my father's, too.

I take off the bracelet and push off the couch. "You tell me you love me, but you're sure not acting like it." I drop the bracelet in his lap as I pass. "I'm going to bed. And don't come to my room, either. I'm locking my door."

With that, I leave him in the theater room. As I climb the stairs, I have tears in my eyes, but I don't cry. Not until I reach my bedroom.

Then I let my sorrow flow.

Chapter 11

When I wake the next morning, it's after eleven. I never sleep this late. Ever.

Then again, I cried until after three o'clock.

And don't my eyes feel it? They're swollen and gummy and feel like I took sandpaper to them.

It's going to be a long day.

Part of me considers pretending I'm sick so I can stay in my room and avoid Gunner. Another part of me wants more than anything to see him so I can search for evidence that his night was as miserable as mine.

I give in and get out of bed. I'll go downstairs, get the lay of the land, and if it doesn't look good, I can pretend to be sick later.

Trudging to the bathroom, I bump into the door as I try to turn the handle, forgetting I locked it last night. Unlocking it, I push it open and switch on the light.

The bracelet is sitting on the marble counter next to the sink. No note. Nothing to indicate he'd been there other than the bracelet.

Tears instantly prickle my eyes, and I turn for the shower.

Playing sick is starting to look more appealing.

I dress in sweatpants and a sweatshirt and dump a bottle of Visine in my eyes. Then I stop at my bedroom door, square my shoulders, and take a deep breath, forcing a smile as I step into the hall.

Wendy's bedroom door is open, and I take a quick peek inside. The bed is made. Gunner isn't there.

Which means he's probably downstairs.

With growing dread, I descend to the living room. Dad is dressed in sweats, and he's watching pregame stats for the college football games that will be on later.

Nick is lying on the couch with his eyes closed. He appears to be sleeping off a hangover. Like Gunner, he's not of legal drinking age, yet, but like me, he's always been responsible. He wouldn't have driven home if he was drunk, which means he drove home hungover this morning or had someone give him a ride. Since his car is in the driveway, my bet is on the former.

I find my mom in the kitchen. She's bright-eyed and bushy-tailed, which means she didn't drink at all last night. Good for her. She's putting together some kind of dip, and the crockpot is churning out the telltale scent of baked beans. She starts them in the crockpot then transfers them to the oven to finish. Her baked beans with pork are just about the best thing on the planet, and we eat them every New Year's Day, along with homemade Reubens. Beans, pork, corned beef, and cabbage. She even bakes a special New Year's cake. My mom goes all out.

I grab the Lucky Charms from the cupboard and round up the milk and a bowl on my way to the breakfast bar.

"Where's Gunner?"

"He left about an hour ago," Mom says, wiping off her hands. "Said he needed to run a few errands before he and Nick leave tomorrow."

"Oh." I dump the cereal into my bowl, spilling some over the side.

"So, did you two have fun last night?"

My gaze shoots to hers. "Last night? What do you mean?" Does she know what he and I did?

She smiles and winks. "After I went to bed. I know you couldn't have gone back to sleep knowing he was in the theater with you. And neither of you look like you got much sleep this morning." She's rattling on, bustling around the kitchen. "So I just assumed the two of you stayed up and watched a movie together."

"No, Mom." I bury my face in my bowl. "I went to bed. I just didn't sleep well. I had nightmares all night."

Ain't that the truth?

"Nightmares?" She pulls the cocoa from the cupboard. It's always been her cure-all for bad dreams. With my mom, it's the little things no one else thinks will help that make a difference. "I'll make you some hot chocolate."

I'm in no mood to argue. Besides, hot chocolate sounds good. "Thanks, Mom."

Bring on the little things. They may be all I have to get me through my heartache.

* * *

Gunner still hasn't returned by three o'clock, and I'm practically clawing my way out of my skin to know where he's gone. At four o'clock, I can't stand his absence, anymore, and have to get out of the house.

I go to Julie's.

By the time I get there, I'm spewing tears like a dysfunctional water fountain.

"What's wrong?" she says once she's hauled me into her bedroom.

"Oh, Julie. Everything." I spill the whole story. All of it. From the first time Gunner snuck into my bedroom, to the first orgasm he gave me, to giving him my V-card, to what we did last night. Then I tell her what happened after that. How we argued and I gave him back the bracelet.

After lightly admonishing me for not telling her sooner about losing my virginity, Julie pulls me into a hug. "Oh, Cami, I'm sorry. Everything will be all right. You'll see."

All I can do is cry. Sob, actually. I'm sleep-deprived, I don't know where he is, and I feel like everything I've always wanted has caved in around me like a sand castle in a hurricane. If my emotional state isn't comprised of a toxic cocktail right now, I don't know what is.

Julie consoles me a little longer, and then I check the time. I have to get back home. Mom will kill me if I miss dinner.

"Call me later, okay?" Julie says, hugging me at the door.

"Okay. Do I look all right? Can you tell I've been crying?" I brush back my hair and blink. I used more Visine to take the red out of my eyes, because I don't want my mom to know I've been bawling my eyes out.

Julie smiles unconvincingly. "Just don't cry on the way home and you'll be fine."

I meander to my car, repeating my new mantra, "I will not cry, I will not cry," all the way home.

* * *

Gunner still isn't at my house when I return home. And he doesn't show up for dinner.

After we eat, Nick leaves to spend the night with Missy. He doesn't even try to hide that he won't be home until morning. Funny how he can be so blatant about the fact that he and Missy are having sex, and yet Gunner can't even tell anyone he likes me.

"Tell Gunner to be ready to go by ten o'clock,"

Nick says as he walks out the door.

The best Christmas vacation of my life has turned into the worst, and now my heart is breaking that he'll be gone in — I check the clock — less than fifteen hours.

"We'll tell him, honey," my mom calls after him.

The house grows quiet except for the sound of the game on TV. I don't even know who's playing. I don't care.

I curl up on the couch and close my eyes.

A short while later, just as I'm on the verge of falling asleep, I hear the back door open and close. I instinctively know it's Gunner and sit up, looking toward the back of the house.

Gunner walks cautiously into the kitchen from the back hallway, looking around as if he's inspecting the landscape before coming farther inside. He's carrying a bouquet of roses. When his gaze finds mine, his shoulders lift and square, and he takes an emboldened step forward.

My pulse quickens. Anticipation wells in my soul as I watch him cross the room.

Entering the living room, he clears his throat again. My mom and dad turn.

"Oh, hi, Gunner. We were wondering where—" My mom cuts off, eyeing the roses curiously before glancing at me with a glimmer of hope. "Uh . . . where you were," she finishes.

My dad frowns, but not in a mean or angry way. More in a what's-this-all-about? kind of way.

Gunner remains standing, his gaze searching mine with something close to conviction.

"Mr. and Mrs. Coombs," he says, "I wanted to, uh . . . I'd like to talk to you about something."

"Honey," my mom says to my dad, "turn down the TV, please."

He does and sits forward in his chair, looking from me to Gunner. Somehow he knows this has to do with me. "What is it you want to tell us, son?"

Gunner squares his shoulders and lifts his chin. "I'm in love with your daughter, sir."

My mom's mouth falls open, and her gaze dances to mine, shining delightfully. I think the only thing that would make her happier right now is if Nick were to return home with Missy and announce that he just asked her to marry him and she said yes.

My dad's a tougher customer. But I can tell he's happy. He's always liked Gunner and his family. There are a lot worse options out there, and he knows I just struck gold with Gunner. But he won't let Gunner off that easily. "You think you love my daughter, son?"

Not to be deterred, Gunner shakes his head. "No, sir. I don't *think* I do. I *know* I do. I'm in love with her." He turns to me. "Cameron, I've loved you for a long time, and I'm sorry it's taken me this long to get my head out of my ass"—he shoots my parents an apologetic glance—"um, sorry, what I meant to say is—"

"It's okay, son," my dad says, biting back a smile. "You're doing good. Go on." He motions for Gunner to get back to his confession.

Red-faced, Gunner turns back to me and steps closer. "Cameron, I know I haven't said the right things in the past couple of days, but I'm in love with you, and I'm not afraid to say it. Not to your parents, not to the world, not even to your brother. Let him kick my ass. It'll be worth it if it means I can hold your hand in public." He kneels in front of me and extends the bouquet of roses, looking at them like he's embarrassed. "I looked everywhere for an open florist, but there's not a lot of places open on New Year's Day. I found these at a convenience store a couple of towns over."

Surely, he hadn't spent all day looking for flowers.

"They're perfect," I say, taking them and drawing them up to my nose. "Absolutely perfect." He could have handed me a bouquet of dandelions for all I care.

His smile warms the shadows of his striking face. "You deserve better."

I shake my head. "It's the thought, Gunner." I close my eyes and sniff the lightly wilted roses then turn my gaze back to his. "I don't need expensive flowers when the thought is the only thing that matters."

He smiles and sits down next to me, wrapping his hand around mine as I lean my head against his shoulder.

My dad turns the sound back up on the TV, and both he and my mom try to act like they're completely unaware of the romance blooming on the corner of the couch where I'm snuggled against Gunner.

"I'm sorry," he whispers, brushing his lips over my hair.

I squeeze his hand and whisper back, "Me, too. Thank you for giving me back the bracelet."

"It's yours. I bought it for you."

I smile and tuck my nose back inside one of the rosebuds.

Yes, it *is* mine. The bracelet and all its little charms. Tiny charms that a lifetime of thought went into.

Little things.

But little things that add up to something big.

Chapter 12

The next morning, I put on the bracelet and, with a spring in my step, join Gunner at the top of the stairs. We descend hand in hand, no longer worried about what my family thinks of our relationship. All but Nick. He hasn't returned home, yet, so he still doesn't know.

Gunner's bags are packed and sitting by the back door, but I can't find it in me to be sad. I'm too happy about going public to be sad.

Mom sets breakfast in front of us.

"What's that?" She gestures toward my wrist.

I lift my arm, showing off the bracelet. "My Christmas gift from Gunner."

My mom examines each charm as Gunner explains them one by one She gets a little misty-eyed at some of the memories his charms represent.

"Oh, Gunner, it's a lovely gift." She circles the counter and hugs him. Then she hugs me. "I'm so happy for the two of you. I always thought you'd make a cute couple."

She pulls back, studying us, and then points in the

direction of the laundry room. "Since Nick will be home any minute, I'll leave you two alone so you can say good-bye." She takes a step back then addresses Gunner. "But you have to promise to go to Saint Martin with us on spring break. We're taking the whole family."

"Um . . ." Gunner glances at me.

I nod. "Missy's going, too."

"Okay," he says. "But I have to pay my own way."

"Nonsense." My mom waves her hand. "You'll be our guest."

Gunner knows better than to argue with my mom, so he concedes the point. "I'm looking forward to it."

"Good. I'll make the arrangements." With a wink at me, she disappears down the back hall, in the direction of the laundry room.

"Looks like you've won over my parents," I say as he takes my hand.

"They're easy. It's Nick I'm worried about."

"Come on." I hop off my barstool and give him a tug. "I don't want to think about my brother right now."

I lead him upstairs to my bedroom. He closes the door then joins me on the bed, where he lies down behind me and wraps me in his arms. We spent a lot of time in my bed while he was home. It will be awhile before I can go to bed again without anticipating his quiet footsteps padding across the carpet as he sneaks into my room.

"You've applied to Ohio State, right?" he asks. Hope pulls at his words.

We're back to this conversation. "Didn't we talk about this already?"

He hugs me tighter, kissing my cheek. "Yes, but you never said you'd applied to Ohio."

"This is really important to you, isn't it?" I tease.

"Quit stalling. Did you apply or not?"

"Yes." I wrap my arms around his. "I applied to Ohio State."

His head tips against the back of mine. "Good. Then we can be together next year. We could probably even get an apartment on campus and —"

"Hey, don't push your luck with my parents. They love you, but I'm not sure they would go for us living together. Besides, you still haven't told Nick about us."

"Only because he wasn't here last night."

"You're not still worried about him kicking your ass, are you?"

"No."

"Are you sure?"

He flips me over and rolls on top of me, stealing my breath. "Are we going to spend the last few minutes we have together talking about Nick or saying good-bye?"

"I don't want to say good-bye." The sadness finally hits me.

"I don't either, but I have to go soon."

"I know." Tears burn my eyes.

"Ssshh." He kisses me. It's just a light kiss, but he lingers, as if he's drinking in my essence, memorizing it.

I lift my head off my pillow and strengthen the connection.

His lips part with mine, and the comfort we've come to find with each other fuses our hearts into one.

All too soon, Nick yells up the stairs, "Gunner! Let's go! Time to blow out of here!"

Gunner groans, breaking our kiss. "Vacation over."

I nod, hating how cold it feels when he pushes himself away from my body.

Taking his hand, I follow him out of my bedroom and back downstairs. My mom is outside hugging Nick. He's already got Gunner's bags in the driveway along with his. When he lets go of Mom, he starts tossing everything into the back of his car.

I exchange glances with Gunner as he lets go of my hand and steps outside. It's now or never.

"There you are," Nick says, catching sight of him. "Let's shake." He slams the trunk of the car and makes for the driver's seat.

"Hold up a second," Gunner says, stopping Nick in his tracks.

Nick watches him over the top of the car. "What's wrong?"

"Nothing's wrong."

"Then let's go. We're late." Nick pulls open the driver's side door, but Gunner remains planted by my side.

"Gunner, what the hell? Let's go."

"I, uh . . ." Gunner glances at me. Then he looks back at Nick. "I just wanted to thank you and your family for letting me stay with you over the break."

Nick stares at him as if he can't believe that's what Gunner wanted to tell him. "Okay," he says, as if he's talking to a small child. "That's great. You're welcome."

"Yeah," Gunner says, "it was cool of everyone to put up with me for the last three weeks, and uh, well, I just wanted to say thank you. And by the way, I'm dating your sister." He wraps his hand around mine.

Nick blinks a few times then just stares at him.

Gunner pulls me closer. "In fact, I'm in love with her. I just wanted you to know that."

Nick's perplexed gaze passes from Gunner to me and back. Then he barks out a laugh. "Well, it's about fucking time."

"Nicolas!" my mom says.

I exchange confused glances with Gunner. "Wait . . . you're not mad?" I ask, looking back at Nick.

"Are you kidding?" Nick laughs again. "I've been wondering how long it was going to take for this douche canoe to get his head out of his ass to ask you out. He's obviously had the hots for you since we were kids." Nick comes around the car and sticks out his hand. Gunner takes it, and Nick pulls him into a man hug, clapping him on the back. "About damn time, Gun. Jesus, I was beginning to think it would never happen. Now, let's go." He gestures toward the car. "You two can suck face next time we come home."

My mouth drops open, and my mom laughs.

Gunner's face flames red as he grins impishly then bends to give me a chaste good-bye kiss. "I'll call you later."

I nod and fight back tears as he lets go of me and climbs into the passenger seat.

I already miss him, but at least now everyone knows we're a couple.

"I'll see you on spring break," he says, holding his arm out the open window.

I take his hand and give it a squeeze, nodding, forcing myself not to cry. "How am I going to get through not seeing you until then?"

"Same way I will," he says as Nick puts the car in gear. "Lots of video chatting, phone calls, and texts. Maybe I'll even send you a card or two."

"I'd like that." I let go of his hand as the car begins to pull away.

"Bye, sis!" Nick calls. "I'll take care of him for you, don't worry."

"You'd better," I yell.

Gunner holds my gaze until they pull out of the driveway and disappear around the bend in the road.

Tears trail down my cheeks, but I'm happy. Really, I am, but spring break can't get here soon enough.

My mom's gentle voice breaks the silence. "You didn't keep the bathroom door locked, did you?"

The air rushes from my lungs as fear grips my gut. I whip my gaze to hers. "Mom, I—"

She's smiling. I wasn't expecting to see a smile on her face.

"I'm not mad," she says.

"You're not?"

"I'm under no illusions, honey. You're eighteen. You're a young woman. I know how things are." She takes my hand and squeezes. "Just promise you're being careful."

In other words, she wants to make sure I'm practicing safe sex.

I nod. "I am."

"Good." She wraps her arm around my shoulders. We stare at the empty street for a long time, until finally my mom pulls me against her in a brief one-armed hug. "I don't know about you, but I could use a cup of hot chocolate."

I turn my gaze to hers. She has tears in her eyes.

She and I are the same height. When did that happen? It seems like only yesterday when I was just a little girl who only reached her hip.

"Hot chocolate sounds good," I say.

As she wipes her eyes, she gives me a little tug in the direction of the back door. "Come on, I'll make you a cup."

I lean into her shoulder and use my sleeve to blot the tears from my cheeks as I stare at my bracelet. The bracelet that's so small but means so much. Each tiny charm represents a different piece of Gunner's heart, and as the miles slowly widen between us, this simple bracelet will keep us connected. It's our lifeline between one another.

"I'd like that, Mom." I let her turn me toward the back door and guide me inside.

After all, it's the little things that matter the most.

And it's the little things that will get me through until I see Gunner again.

Until I can see him every day.

Until I walk down the aisle with him and become his wife.

But that's years away. Until then, I'm going to enjoy all those little things Gunner and I have yet to share. Little things that will someday grow into the greatest gift of all.

From the Author

Thank you for reading Little Things. If you enjoyed this story, please consider leaving a review at the retail site of your choice or on Goodreads to help other readers discover the book.

Now, turn the page for an excerpt from Good Karma, the first book in my Strong Karma Trilogy, and the silver medalist in the 2016 eLit Awards for Best Erotic Fiction.

Excerpt from Good Karma

She read the card. Her heart performed another perfect swan dive into the pit of her stomach, and she glanced warily at him.

"Go ahead," he said. "I can already tell this one's good."

He had no idea.

"Okay, um…" She looked back down. *Here goes.* "Take me to a place in the house where we haven't had sex." Her gaze flicked nervously to his before she continued. "Kiss me…and then whisper what you would do to me if we were to…get it on there." She lowered the card to her lap and kept her head down.

Mark waited a moment then lifted her foot from between his legs, leaned toward her, and reached for her hand. Without looking at him, she took it. As he moved into the middle of the couch, he tugged her onto his lap and situated her so that she faced him. Her legs straddled his thighs.

Her heart beat like a wild drum in her chest.

"Come here," he whispered, caressing her cheek in such a way that drew her face to his. His lips found hers and held them in a static kiss. He didn't move, and neither did she. All that mattered was the simple, chaste connection and the way a thousand tiny starbursts exploded throughout her body. His kiss seemed so innocent, and yet it sent shards of erotic desire into her blood.

He broke away, but held her close. "Since we haven't had sex, yet, I choose here." He patted the couch. "And as for what I would do to you here, I would make you stand in front of me, where I would slip my hands up your skirt and pull off your panties. I would invite you onto my lap and whisper how sexy you are…" He bent around and kissed her earlobe. "You're *very* sexy."

A shiver raced down her spine.

His lips skimmed down her jaw to her chin. "I would kiss your neck." And he did, letting his tongue sneak out to lick a fiery trail from one side to the other.

Karma felt like she was in a vicious state of sensory overload. She was practically panting.

"And I wouldn't stop making love to you until you came." His breath washed over the skin of her neck, and his lips closed over her shoulder as he licked her. "Your first orgasm with a man inside you," he said a moment later when he met her gaze again.

As badly as she needed oxygen, she could hardly breathe.

"Oh," she whispered breathlessly. Apparently she could barely speak, too.

His gaze dropped to her mouth, and a heartbeat later, their lips meshed again, this time with more force. A quiet groan broke from deep in his chest.

She wrapped her arms around his neck and shoulders. No way was she letting this moment go. All night, they had talked about sex. Visions of him in various states of undress had taunted her throughout their game, and she had felt his magnificence against the sole of her foot for at least ten minutes. They had fallen under the very spell the game was designed to cast, because they were unraveling into lust faster than a stripper takes off her clothes.

"Bite my lip," he muttered against her mouth. "Let yourself go."

She thought she *had been* letting go, but clearly he knew her better than she knew herself, because the moment he told her to let go, she found a fifth gear she hadn't thought possible. Her tongue danced with his, and he groaned low and loud, and when she did as he asked and took his bottom lip between her teeth, he practically growled, and his fingers curled into claws on her back, pulling her closer.

"That's my girl," he said when she released his lip. Then he assaulted her mouth again, nipping her lip as if to show her the pleasure she had just given him. And it *was* pleasurable. Being bitten, even if only lightly, knocked her good side clear out of the picture, leaving only the vixen she had discovered in Chicago.

Passion rose in her blood, turning her into someone else. She was no longer sweet, shy, good Karma. She was lusty, sultry, bad Karma. A woman lost to her desires, driven by erotic need, who wanted to experience pleasure only a man could give. That only *Mark* could give.

He pulled away, and she opened her eyes to find

him grinning at her, his gaze hooded.

"What?" she said, breathless.

His left eyebrow twitched. "You're pulling my hair."

She glanced up and found that her hands had curled into fists, and tufts of his dark brown hair poked out between her fingers. She quickly opened her hands and let go.

Of course, this made Mark laugh. "I wasn't complaining. Remember, I like when a woman pulls my hair."

"Uh, yes..." She sheepishly looked away. "I got a bit carried away."

He pulled her down so that her forehead rested against his. "I know. And I liked it. A lot."

For a long moment, nothing was said as Mark ran his palms slowly up and down her back. "I want to be the first man to show you what you've been missing, Karma," he said softly. "I want to succeed where others have failed."

Her bashful side made a subtle reappearance, and she curled in on herself. "Why?"

He caressed her cheek. "For one, I think you deserve to know what a really good orgasm feels like, don't you?"

When he put it that way, how could she say no?

His fingertips brushed back her hair. "Second of all, I'm a man. And, like most men, I'm proud and have a big ego. I'm not afraid to admit it. And when I make a woman feel good...when I give her such intense pleasure that she screams my name as she's falling into the most unbelievable orgasm she's ever had, I take great pride in that." He hesitated and narrowed his eyes. "Especially when I know she's never felt anything like that before." He paused to let his words sink in.

Karma's entire body heated. They had most definitely sunk in.

Who says egomania is a bad thing?

Mark shifted against the couch, and she felt his erection press against her. "To know that I awakened that part of a woman gives me tremendous satisfaction, Karma. It's the best ego boost in the world." His gaze danced back and forth between her eyes. "So, the most direct answer to your question is that I want to feel you fall apart and come undone under my touch." He took a shaky breath and closed his palm over her cheek. "My God, but just the thought of that...to see you, head thrown back, that heart-shaped mouth open as you cry out..." He rubbed his thumb over her bottom lip. "Let's just say the idea turns me on very much."

The idea turned her on, too, as in way on.

"There's something undeniably sexy about you, Karma," he said. "You intrigue me, and I want the pleasure of discovering you, and of helping you discover yourself if you'll let me. Will you? Let me?"

As the air in the room froze and her heart beat in a

wild rhythm, hope and anxious anticipation broke over Mark's expression. His intense stare never wavered.

The most lascivious aspect of their pending affair pressed solidly against the apex of her body, and she had to force herself not to rotate her hips. How would he feel inside her? What would it feel like to finally have an orgasm — a *real* orgasm — during intercourse? Mark promised to answer all those questions and more.

What he was offering was more than she ever could have imagined. He was handsome, charming, intelligent, and confident in his abilities. He was the kind of man women dream of. And he wanted to be with her. *Her!*

If you want to change some things in your life, you need to change some things in your life.

"Yes," she whispered. "Yes, I'll let you."

She bit her lip and a shudder danced up her spine as he smiled.

Mark had to be a magician, because only a magician could have made her behave the way she had tonight.

This was going to be good. So very, very good. She didn't regret her decision to wear that gold brooch to work today one bit. Not one damn bit.

About the Author

Donya Lynne is the bestselling author of the award winning All the King's Men and Strong Karma Series and a member of Romance Writers of America. Making her home in a wooded suburb north of Indianapolis with her husband, Donya has lived in Indiana most of her life and knew at a young age she was destined to be a writer. She started writing poetry in grade school and won her first short story contest in fourth grade. In junior high, she began writing romantic stories for her friends, and by her sophomore year, she'd been dubbed *Most Likely to Become a Romance Novelist*. In 2012, she fulfilled her dream by publishing her first two novels and a novella. In 2016, she began writing serialized novels under the pen name, Dick Hertz. Her work has earned her two IPPYs, three ELit Awards, a USA Today Recommended Read, and numerous accolades. In October and November of 2015, she had two books hit the Smashwords Top 25 Bestsellers list. When she's not writing, she can be found cheering on the Indianapolis Colts or doing her cats' bidding.

Books by Donya Lynne

All the King's Men Series
Rise of the Fallen
Heart of the Warrior
Micah's Calling
Rebel Obsession
Return of the Assassin
All the King's Men – Prequel
Bound Guardian Angel

Strong Karma Series
Good Karma
Coming Back To You
Full Circle

Standalones
Finding Lacey Moon
Little Things

M/M Standalones
Winter's Fire

Writing as Dick Hertz
Size Matters, Parts 1-8